Montana Trail

Montana Trail

LAURAN PAINE

Sagebrush
Large Print Westerns

Library of Congress Cataloging-in-Publication Data

Paine, Lauran.
  Montana trail / Lauran Paine.
     p.   cm.
  ISBN 1-57490-459-0 (alk. paper)
  1. Montana—Fiction. 2. Large type books. I. Title.

PS3566.A34 M658 2003
813'.54—dc21

2002153825

C\ 51952666

Cataloging in Publication Data is available from
the British Library and the National Library of Australia.

Sagebrush Large Print Westerns are published in the United
States and Canada by Thomas T. Beeler, Publisher, PO Box 659,
Hampton Falls, New Hampshire 03844-0659. ISBN 1-57490-459-0

Published in the United Kingdom, Eire, and the Republic of
South Africa by Isis Publishing Ltd, 7 Centremead, Osney
Mead, Oxford OX2 0ES England. ISBN 0-7531-6906-1

Published in Australia and New Zealand by Bolinda Publishing
Pty Ltd, 17 Mohr Street, Tullamarine, Victoria, Australia, 3043
ISBN 1-74030-913-8

Manufactured by Sheridan Books in Chelsea, Michigan.

Montana Trail

1

UNDER A FAINT GRAY DAWN SKY THE STEELY FLOOR OF the world stretched away flat, silent and misty until it fetched up sharp against the knife-like edge of a rising sun. The first rays shot out across the world blood-red, penetrating and irresistible. Where the night mist lingered it was flayed ragged and diluted by that incredibly swift-rushing light. The light lost its redness, turned greeny then turned wrought gold. When it did this it also turned warm.

The lumpy bundle nearest the tinkling little cold creek stirred. A head emerged much like the head of a turtle, turning, lifting, sniffing the air, testing the hour, feeling the new day's pulse and heartbeat. Except, unlike a turtle, this head had spiky light hair standing in every direction and a beard-stubbled youthful face swollen from rest and not yet willing to entirely put aside the warmth and goodness of a buffalo robe bedroll for the chill, sun lighted though it was, of dawn.

Still, someone had to start the cooking fire, carve the side meat, rassle the coffee, then check the horses. Someone always had to do that; a man could ride from here to heaven and every morning on the way someone'd have the chores to do. Well; it could've been worse. It could, for example, have been the dead of a Montana winter when a man's knees and knuckles got locked in place from freezing cold and instead of sunlight upon awakening there'd be a foot of dry snow atop a man's bedding.

In some willows up a nearby draw, dim and ghostly, lingered some of the misty dregs of the night. Up there came the sounds of hobbled horses moving too, which solved one of the yawning cowboy's problems; since there'd be feed up there he would not now have to trouble himself with the animals.

On the thin, cold air came a distant long lowing. It persisted until a garrulous little wavering answer came back then the lowing ceased. Elsewhere, some animal yapped. A dog or perhaps a coyote, or even a little red-eyed fox. The world came awake slowly and reluctantly. One of the blessings of spring was the good cold nights for sleeping and the blessedly warm days for moving about. The trouble with that was simply that Montana's springtimes were totally unpredictable. A sleety wind straight off the Big Horns could come suddenly and whip man and horse from all directions at once.

"Hey," the man called, when he had his fire crackling and his side meat frying. "Hey, you going to sleep all day? It's after five o'clock, the sun's up, the birds are singing, the—"

"Goad dell," came the muffled, deep and gruff growl from under the farthest blanket roll. But gradually, perhaps drawn by the exquisite perfume of coffee and frying bacon in the dawn chill, sharper then, more rewarding than at any other time of day, the second head emerged. This one's hair was as black as midnight, slightly curly so that it didn't stand up spike-like, and when the man reared up on his elbows tossing back his blankets he looked thicker, heavier-boned, than his grinning companion over at the fire.

The light-headed one regarded his friend and grinned. "Good thing I got a strong stomach." He picked up a strip of frying meat with a convenient stick, critically examined it then flopped it over onto its back into the little fry pan. "Maybe, like folks say, things do work out

2

for the best, Matt."

With his wet eyes puckered against all the brilliance of this new day Matt gravely studied their surroundings. His friend went on cooking over there, squatting on his spurred boot heels, tending his bacon and from time to time sipping black coffee from a dented tin cup.

"There's a ranch hereabouts. 'While back I heard a cow bawlin' at a new calf. Maybe running the horses down in the dark last night put us in a fair way of finding work."

Matt made a circuit of the inside of his mouth with his tongue, spat, grunted upright and tugged on his cold boots. If nothing ever wholly awakened a cowboy in a crisp morning, cold boots did. Matt got up, wrinkled his nose at the aroma of food, then went tramping grimly off in the direction of the creek to wash. The only comment he made was an unflattering reference to the horses which had somehow slipped their hobbles the previous evening and had bolted. It had required four hours of tracking by moonlight to find them again, in this forlorn spot, and neither Matthew Grady nor his pardner Emmett Ray had the slightest notion where they were.

But, as Emmett reflected, squatting comfortably by his fire, they wouldn't have known anyway, even if they'd made that trek with their saddles on their own backs for a change, in broad daylight. This Montana country was new to them both.

Emmett poured a cup of coffee, set it atop a flat stone and divvied up the side meat into two old tin plates. Breakfast was ready. Down in Colorado the boys had said anyone traveling up the Montana trail would punch a couple of new holes in his belt before he got to decent food again, meaning that the trail was long and the land big. Emmett could now sagely confirm both those

3

prognostications.

He'd been on short rations before though. So had Matt. In fact, as he sipped his coffee and chewed his side meat, he philosophized pleasantly that being hungry got to be a way of life after a while; a man even adjusted to it and expected nothing else. Fellers died from too much grub and they died of not enough, but who ever heard of anyone dying of just barely enough?

Matt came back fresh-scrubbed and bright-eyed. "That creek's colder'n a witch's kiss," he muttered, picked up the cup off its little flat stone and gulped down his first drink of coffee. Emmett said nothing; when you'd traveled back trails with a man as long as these two had been scuffing around together, you got to know exactly when to talk and when not to. This was a 'not to' time. Give the java five minutes then the whole world would brighten. Funny, but that's how it was with some men.

Matt squatted, shifted his hip holster so the gun wouldn't gouge, picked up his tin plate and ate. "Ever get so blamed mad at a horse you could shoot it?" He inquired.

"Lots of times," replied Emmett. "The trouble is, whenever I've felt that mean I've always been so far from anywhere that the danged horse was all that stood between me'n a hundred-mile walk. So I've never shot one."

Matt's interest perked up. He was a sturdy man with eyes as black as his hair, smooth dark hide and big white teeth as even though carved of ivory. He moved with an almost cat-like grace. He had a way of looking at things that was penetratingly sharp and observant. Someone seeing Matthew Grady for the first time wouldn't have had any trouble at all pegging him for what he was. A range rider proficient at his trade, a bad man to cross, direct in his dealings and as tough, as

4

resilient, as a horsehide boot.

Emmett shared two things with Matt; they were both an even six feet tall and they both had the same look of top-hand efficiency. Their coloring as well as their builds were different. Matt was heavy-boned, powerfully muscled-up and somehow gave an impression of restlessness. Emmett on the other hand was whipcord-lean, fair complexioned and showed in just about everything he did a calm sort of philosophical acceptance of things. He had that rare but wonderful ability to grin in almost any circumstances. His eyes were an amiable blue and his long mouth with its tough-set cast, had a slight lilt to its outer edges that disarmed people at once. Folks invariably liked Emmett on sight. With Matt it was different; folks watched him and waited, never sure.

Where the pair of them squatted looking around at this range they'd been unable to discern clearly the night before when they'd trailed their runaway stock here, smoke rose straight up into the winy thin high country air, then curved and floated up that dim, misty draw where their horses drowsed on full bellies. Above that draw, bearing off westerly, to their left, the wall of the lingering night stretched upwards along a mountainside. Everywhere else though, the peaks retreated leaving a huge rolling plain turned dark green this time of the year with grass and brush and occasionally, with budding trees.

Westerly, where the sunlight was just beginning its ascent up through the purple-tiered old trees on the mountain slope, there stood a high peak with a snowfield at its apex. Here, when the sunlight finally hit, the rocks turned tawny brown, the snowfield turned pale pink, and the endless ranks of marching trees going

5

blindly on uphill, assumed a dark shade of reddish purple.

"Big country," stated Matt, refilling his cup from the coffee pot. "Good grass and browse too. You're probably right, Em; there's a cow outfit somewhere up in here. But you know—this'd be a hell of a land to hang around in, come wintertime."

Emmett poured the grease atop their tiny fire, which flared wildly and put up an oily smoke, then bent to cleaning the fry pan with switches of grass and dirt. "Kill the rest of that coffee," he said, jutted his chin eastward where the prairie had full rein as the mountains fell away until they were little more than a hazy hint upon the farthest curve of earth. "Should be a town over there somewhere." He then paused to consider his own words and added: "But wherever there's plenty of water folks'd put towns anywhere they pleased."

Matt, gazing across his pardner's shoulder at that dark mountainside, filled his cup for the third time just by feel, then gently put aside the pot and held the cup without raising it, his black eyes drawing down into a shrewd, narrowed line. "We got callers," he said softly. "Must have been the smoke."

Emmett whirled half around. He saw them come straggling out of the gloomy trees far back and counted their numbers. "Five," he pronounced. "Seedy lookin' lot."

Matt tossed off the coffee and shrugged. "What'd you expect? We take their land, kill their game, pollute their streams and when they get sore we shoot 'em. Pretty hard for men to keep their self-respect under those circumstances."

"Not so hard," contradicted Emmett, watching those distant small figures start to bunch up and ride their

6

horses at a slow walk as they approached. "Injuns can salve their self-respect awful easy when they find two whites alone like this."

Matt, studying those oncoming horsemen, sighed. "Better make some more java," he said. "Look like a little hunting party."

"Or scalping party," muttered Emmett, turning to take the coffee pot back for fresh water at creekside.

Matt's black eyes drifted to Emmett's back as the fairer man hiked off. He grinned. Emmett never trusted redskins. There hadn't been an Indian war in twenty years and he'd shared pup-stew in as many camps as Matt had but he still didn't trust Indians. Well; there were always plenty of reasons for distrust—but they lay on *both* sides, not just one side.

Matt stood up, tilted down his hatbrim to keep out the glare, and watched their guests come closer. Five armed Indian hunters on ponies still shedding their winter hair and looking about as wild and natural with that gloomy backdrop mountain at their backs as they could ever have looked.

The men themselves were tall, flat-boned dark and aquiline. The closer they got the more they showed that peculiar gaminess which was part of their ancient heritage. They were hunters now, to be sure, but their fathers had been much more; they had been drinkers of the wind, the *ozuye we tawatas,* the Men of War in this land of the high sky and the big land.

Emmett came back, poked at his fire and set the pot atop its stones, stood up swiftly and faced around. The Indians were less than a gunshot off now, clearly visible in all aspects. One of them had a bloody piece of soiled canvas tied aft of his saddle. All of them rode with Winchester rifles balanced across their laps. One of

7

them, an older man, had braids but the others wore their hair short. Their attire was mostly range dress; butternut shirts, denim pants, boots, spurs, soiled old broad-brimmed hats. But one had a droopy feather in his hatband and another had a smoke-tanned short riders' coat with fringe, loosely across his wide shoulders and thick chest. They were motley and unsmiling and intently watchful as they crossed that last hundred yards, their midnight-black eyes missing nothing at all.

2

MATT AND EMMETT WERE FROM CROW AND Shoshoni country. These were Sioux bucks, obviously, and to address them in Crow would be equivalent to calling down upon a Protestant minister a stout Catholic blessing. But everyone knew a few words of lakota or dahkota.

Matt said: *"How kola,"* and afterwards traded looks with the five redskins with Emmett standing loose and easy, his right hand just happening to be draped across the black-rubber butt of his .45.

The buck with the braids, older than the others, lined of face and with eyes that never stopped moving, said, *"How kola, Wasicun."* Hello, whiteman. He didn't grin but two of the others did. One swung out and down, his spurs making the only sound. He kept grinning, his dark glance mischievous. He brushed a clenched fist across his chest, opened two fingers and passed the hand from right to left—from north to south. "Heap big white cowboys," he solemnly exclaimed, "off reservation for white cowboys."

One of the other men laughed, throwing his head far

8

back to do this. They all laughed then, except the braided one, Emmett didn't even smile but in Matt Grady's black stare a hard glimmer of understanding showed.

"Hey, bronco," he said to the hand-talking buck. "You want a cup of java, or you want a fight?"

The flat-boned, tough Indian's laughter went away but his stare at Matt remained pixieish. "Aw hell," he said, the only difference in his talk and Matt's being a sort of guttural clipped pronouncement of the words, "It's too early in the morning to fight. Besides, we smelt that coffee three miles back." He turned to Emmett, and here his very black glance turned gradually sober. It is the way with men attuned through heritage to naturalness to correctly gauge another man's mood instantly. Emmett was ill at ease; he didn't care much for Indians. To him, the Sioux said, "We've got a saddle of buckmeat and seven blue grouse." It was an offer of friendship; it could have been taken no other way among red men or white men. Emmett lifted his right hand as though he hadn't really known it had been on his holstered gun at all.

"The java'll be ready directly it boils," he said. "We've already eaten but you're welcome to the fire."

Three of the hunters went back to get slices of the meat. The braided one and the spokesman walked on over to squat by the fire and stir new life into it with more faggots. The spokesman kept turning now and then to gaze upwards where Matt stood. Finally this one stood up and said, "I'm Black Cloud. They call me Blackie." He stood waiting.

Matt nodded over towards Emmett. "Names don't mean a lot, but his name's Emmett Ray. Mine's Matt Grady."

9

The Indian nodded, his alert eyes lingering while he arranged some thoughts. "Crow," he murmured, and raised both eyebrows to make a question of it.

Matt looked straight back without replying.

Emmett moved up as the other hunters came forward with their fry pan and their meat. The coffee was boiling. He said to the one called Blackie, "Big country. We're not from around here. Looks like good hunting country."

Emmett was clearly drawing the Sioux's attention away from Matt purposely. The Indian understood and turned to watch his friends set to work making their breakfast.

"Yeah it's a big country," he said quietly. "In the old days it was all hunting country. Better then than now, they tell me." He gazed over where the braided older man was slicing meat with a razor-like knife. "He remembers; he was a kid then but he remembers." Slowly the Sioux looked up again, considering Emmett in a detached manner. "Still better for me than for you. Y'see, when the fall roundups are finished, I ride back into the mountains, find some lodges and hole up. Redskins sort of all hang together nowadays. Not like in his time," nodding towards the braided one. "In his day Indians spent the winters stalkin' each other. Now—no. They all sort of gang together, hunt a little, eat a little, loaf around their camps waitin' for spring. For you—for your pardner—it's the towns."

Matt rummaged for a deflated little tobacco sack as he listened, dropped his head and went to work, black eyes half-closed to slits. The Sioux cast a sidelongs glance around. Emmett hunkered to help with the coffee.

"Any towns around?" he asked.

10

The braided buck, thinking he was being spoken to, looked up, still unsmiling, raised an arm and pointed rigidly northeastward, dropped the arm and forgot all about Emmett as the others crowded up to cook and eat and drink coffee.

"Any cow outfits hirin' yet?" Emmett asked, twisting to look at Blackie.

"A little early," the Sioux said. "Another couple weeks maybe. Still, if you fellers went in early you might get hired on." He made a wild gesture. "All this country belongs to Doc Farraday. Biggest cowman south of the Big Horn river." He wrinkled his nose in a small, wry grin. "Farraday's a rich man; he doesn't like hunters on his land. He doesn't even like strange riders crossin' it."

Matt, quietly smoking, said, "You mean like us?"

Blackie nodded. "Yeah. Like you—an also like us. That's why we finally come out of the trees back there. We saw your smoke, knew damned well you were strangers, an' rode on down. If you'd been Farraday's men we wouldn't have let them see us. But you were strangers. That was plenty obvious. Otherwise you'd never have camped here or lit that fire and sent up smoke."

Matt thoughtfully watched the men squatting around the fire eating. "Sounds like a real jolly feller—this Doc Farraday, Blackie. Sounds like he's mean."

Blackie accepted an upheld limp piece of cooked meat on a stick. He bit down hard and chewed. He had something in his mind about Matt; it was uppermost and yet he wouldn't speak of it. He ate for a while, Indian-like, turning many thoughts over and over before coming down to any kind of a decision, and all during this he was silent.

11

"How far to that town?" Emmett asked him.

"Oh; ten miles. Ride northeast. You'll hit the old military road first. Cross it an' keep on riding. You'll see the town this afternoon. But don't loaf. Farraday catches you moseyin' along and he'll raise the devil."

Matt said, "Blackie; how about you an' your friends; he might catch you too."

The Indian's dark gaze showed that mischievous twinkle again. "No chance. This is as far out as we come when we're huntin' over here. We can run back into the forest before anyone can come even close to gettin' us."

"Sure," said Matt, and began to quietly look out and around. When he'd finished making this study he said in the same quiet tone. "Didn't this all used to be Sioux land?"

Blackie nodded. At their feet the braided one looked upwards, his beady gaze fixed hard on Matt. He put his fist sideways to his heart then abruptly flung it outwards as though hurling something from him, which was the *wibluta* hand-talk sign for something being snatched away.

"You understand?" He asked.

Matt didn't answer; he smoked and impassively regarded the older buck, then turned aside to address the younger, standing Indian. "You had it and you lost it," he said, sounding more bitter than scornful of the redmen for losing their empire of high mountains and endless grass. "And that's about the way it's always been—with you or with anyone else. Whites or reds."

Blackie shrugged. In the smoky places of the winter nights he'd heard all the old tales, and if sometimes they stirred in his breast a quick, fierce anger, he wasn't a blanket Indian; he'd been to the log schools, so he knew

12

perfectly well that while old wounds heal slowly, for himself and the bucks of his generation, the old hatred was no good. Besides, he was now as much whiteskin as redskin. School did that; more than just schools though, living in the cow camps, the bunkhouses, the cow towns, with other range riders, taught him that once the old wars were done and over, he and his friends who lived by the saddle, the gun, the long drives were very much alike. It had never occurred to Blackie, though, that as much of the hide-lodge environment of his own people had rubbed off on the white riders as their ways had also rubbed off on him.

What he definitely *did* know was simply that men weren't very different. Oh, it took a lot of time, of strife and heartbreak, agony on both sides for them to locate their final common ground, and no man ever forgot the anguish of his tribe, but only renegades to both sides kept at the hating.

There were five men around the fire. Emmett, the braided one, the other three. One of the younger ones gazed at Emmett, his face still, his liquid black eyes knowing. He said, "They got big hills in Colorado but not like these hills in Montana. Tell you what; if you don't find work at the town, come back up this way— only stay up in the trees were they won't see you. Head up towards that snowfield peak. There's an Injun camp up there. You can sit around, play a little poker, eat good and have a rest. Then later on, head back and find the work."

Emmett nodded. It was a generous offer casually made, always casually made because redskins made light of their most valued things purposefully. No man likes to have his friendship spurned. No man likes to be made a fool of by rejection. "Sure," he muttered to the

Sioux and smiled a little. "How'd you know we came from Colorado?"

"Easy," said another Indian, wiping grease off his square-blunted jaw with a soiled sleeve. "Colorado horses; shed off already. Montana's winters are longer." This one jerked a thumb upwards where Matt was standing with Black Cloud. "Crow," he said. Emmett got busy right away. He filled all their cups until the coffee pot was empty. He stood up and looked around.

"Ten miles; we better be shoving off or we'll never make that town. Hey Matt: You ready?"

Matt dropped his cigarette and nodded. "See you boys again," he said, turning, resting his black glance longest on the Indian who'd wiped his chin. He seemed on the verge of some remark but Emmett called from where he was rolling his bed.

"I got the breakfast, you fetch the horses."

They rigged out under the interested eyes of the Sioux, packed up and got astride. Matt tossed the hunters a loose kind of a nod and started off. Emmett, slower at his chores, was just mounting. Blackie strolled over.

"What's he got to be ashamed about? Hell, Emmett; it's worse being all Injun than only half. When you're half that entitles you to half the respect. Anyway fellers don't go around wearin' feathers any more or rushin' out Injun huntin' when there's nothin' else to do."

Emmett leaned a little and earnestly said, "Blackie, you're probably a good hand. Only someday you're goin' to have to learn—all men got their private feelings."

"Well, all right. But he's still half Crow isn't he?"

Emmett nodded. "Yeah, he's half Injun—Crow Injun."

14

"Well hell, Emmett, this is ancient Sioux hunting land. But we didn't haul him down and slit his nostrils for trespassin' did we? Then if we can make it why can't he?"

"He can. He just's got this little touchiness is all."

Blackie turned to gaze out where Matt was riding along. "He better get over it. Someday he'll get touchy at the wrong time—with the wrong man."

Now Emmett straightened back. Now he was upon firm ground again. "Don't you never bet on that, Blackie. I've been ridin' with him four years now. Don't you never figure any livin' man's goin' to walk over that one."

Blackie's obsidian eyes lifted, turned speculative and skeptical. "That tough, eh?" He murmured. "Well maybe. All I got to go on is what the old-timers told me, and they say never was a Crow born a Sioux couldn't whip with one hand tied back."

Emmett's genial lips parted in a slow and wolfish smile. "Good thing you didn't put it to a test, pardner. Good thing you didn't. Well; were obliged for your company. See you again sometime, maybe."

Emmett rode on. He had that gamy smell in his nostrils, though, even after he caught up with Matt and they went quietly along for a couple of miles with the good morning sunshine loosening their muscles. Matt seemed to have forgotten the hunters as he swung his head left and right.

"Sure good country," he said conversationally. "This Doc Farraday knew a good thing when he saw it. But the trick was to be on hand at the right time, I think."

"Suppose we don't find work at this town, Matt. You want to go back and tent up for a while with those fellers?"

15

Matt looked ironic. "Set up our own camp," he said. "Better huntin' when there's just the two of us to feed."

Emmett considered the onward ocean of new grass for some sign of the town. He didn't find it but he did sight a thin long line of horsemen out there a mile off moving towards him like tiny cloud shadows that grew and diminished as the light played over them.

"Matt; if those hunters weren't spoofin', up yonder there ridin' all sprung out towards us, comes trouble. Farraday riders more'n likely."

Grady looked ahead, said nothing for a long time and kept studying the men they were heading straight for. They had been seen, obviously, and the fanned out way those rangemen were coming meant that they intended interception. Matt blew out a ragged big breath. "What's the matter with this Farraday, anyway?" he said sounding annoyed. "What harm can two sets of horse tracks do across his lousy range?"

"You've seen the type before," replied Emmett, reaching down to ease off the little buckskin thong that slipped over the hammer of his .45 and kept it from rolling out of the hip holster. "They got their empires and they run 'em like they were the Lord A'mighty. The thing is—there are four of 'em, so we don't argue none. Besides that, bein' strangers can hurt us if we get to arguin', just like it can help us if we just say we're sorry an' let it go at that."

Matt snorted. "Those Sioux back there—ten thousand years on this land, then overnight one mossback stakes his claim an' makes 'em skulk around in a lousy forest like they were skulking thieves. Turns a man's stomach."

The fanned out cowboys suddenly halted. It was clear to them the pair of oncoming strangers did not intend to run away.

16

3

THERE WERE TWO ON THE LEFT, TWO ON THE RIGHT, and one thick-shouldered burly individual in a blanket coat in the center. It was this burly man who sat there ramrod-stiff looking down his hooked and high-bridged nose at Emmett and Matt, who seemed to be the headman of this crew.

Matt rode up to within a hundred feet, reined down to a halt and put both his hands atop the saddlehorn, looking just as coldly at the burly man as all five of those horsemen were staring at him and Emmett.

The riders were a raunchy lot, yeasty, a little greasy around the middle like permanent riders get in the wintertime, plenty capable looking. The burly man with his blanket coat turned up around his neck even though it was warm now, several hours after sunrise, was seamed of face and marked by a life that had rarely been easy. Besides his high-bridged hawkish nose he had steely grey eyes that seemed from long habit to look down on other men. Their expression was distant, aloof, cold, like the set of the burly man's thin-lipped slash of a mouth.

Emmett smiled. " 'Mornin'," he said. No one answered. No one smiled back. Emmett's grin got hung up. "Just passin' through. We been told there's a town northeastward. Thought we'd head on over and see about work."

The burly man spoke, ignoring lanky Emmett and concentrating his entire attention upon Matt. "This is Farraday range. No trespassing allowed."

"Didn't see any signs," replied Matt without any inflexion. He and the burly man were measuring one another like dogs prancing stiff-legged around each other, hackles up.

"There aren't any signs. There don't have to be. I'm Doc Farraday and I'm telling you—no trespassing."

Matt said, "I never go where I'm not wanted, Mister Farraday. We'll head off your range straight as an arrow."

Farraday accepted this but he wasn't quite satisfied. Matthew Grady interested him. Emmett saw the toughness of his face break a little with grudging wonderment.

"Where you from?" Farraday asked.

"Colorado."

"What brought you to Montana?"

"We've never been here before. Thought we might ride up and work a season; get a look at the land." Matt gently waggled his head left to right. "Seems like we made a mistake though. The land looks good—the people in it don't."

Emmett quickly said, "Mister Farraday; what's the name of the town we're makin' for?"

Farraday didn't answer. He didn't even look at Emmett. His tough face got a locked-on expression of antagonism. To Matt he said quietly, "Maybe the people in this country don't try to look pleasant to drifters and bums. Maybe they've got enough riff-raff pokin' around uninvited on their ranges already, cowboy; enough saddle tramps eatin' free beef up the hidden canyons."

Matt lifted his left hand, the one with his reins in it. He looked at Farraday's riders a moment then back to the cowman. "Big talk an' big odds, Mister Farraday. We'll let it pass. Still, I'm glad we met. Em an' I sort of figured we might look you up for a job. Now that we've seen you—heard you—I guess we know better. Let's

18

get along, Em."

Emmett also raised his rein hand to ride along. Farraday's slaty eyes smouldered. For a second Emmett thought he was going to say something to halt them, but he didn't. He simply turned a little in the saddle and watched them ride on. Matt set his course to pass between those two cowboys on the left. There really wasn't that much room but Matt didn't change course. Emmett, behind and perhaps twenty feet back, followed Matt.

The cowboys watched Matt. One of them raised his hand as though to give way but the other one growled something and sat like stone, dark brows rolling downward. This one wasn't going to give an inch. Matt pressed right on into that too-narrow space. To Emmett the whole thing was senseless. In the first place there was a hundred miles of empty land in every direction, Matt didn't have to deliberately force a passage between those two men like that. In the second place, Farraday and his crew looked mean.

But Matt kept on until his stirrup hooked the stirrup of the darkly scowling man. He halted, leaned a little off his cantle-board and said to the range rider, "Mister; slack off."

"Who says?" Snarled the cowboy, dropping his right hand down the off side.

Matt, with both hands atop the horn, shook his head. "Don't do anything rash like goin' for your gun. I'll knock half your teeth out if you do."

Emmett eased his own right hand down. This was a very bad moment. He and Matt had their backs to Farraday and on the other side sat two more riders, watchful and prepared.

Farraday unexpectedly said, "Slack off, Mike. Let

'em on through."

Emmett scarcely believed his ears. He wanted the worst way to look around at the bitter-faced cattleman but he didn't dare; not at least until he saw whether Mike was going to obey or not. Mike obeyed. He reined off and let Matt pass on. As Emmett also passed through he finally did turn to look back. Doc Farraday was sitting his horse like a statue, regarding Matt's back with an odd expression across his face.

They were half a mile on before Matt turned and said, as though nothing at all had happened back there, "He never did tell you the name of the town, Em."

Emmett was thinking of something else. "You know what that Blackie feller told me back there? He said someday you're goin' to get raunchy at the wrong time with the wrong man. By gawd Matt I believe him. What the hell's got into you, anyway? You've been actin' mean as a bobcat ever since breakfast."

Matt grinned. Shrewd lines showed like crows feet at the outer edges of his black eyes. His lips curled back to show perfectly formed large white teeth. "Well; everybody we've met so far in this damned country's got a big bump of curiosity and a chip on his shoulder. Em, you know for a fact a man shouldn't go tramplin' over another man's sensitivities just because he's riding over a stretch of private grass."

"Yeah," muttered Emmett right back, his voice dry and clipped. "I know somethin' else too. You better quit puttin' gunpowder in your grub; it'll make you so mean I'll be buryin' you one of these days."

Matt chuckled, turned slack in the saddle as the sun steadily mounted, and for a long time the pair of them rode along saying nothing, only watching how the land subtly changed. The mountains took off on a northward tangent which sometimes cut sharply eastward. Their retreat was quick and abrupt leaving more and more prairie visible as the horsemen passed, putting even the long shadows farther off on their left.

They eventually struck a road, crossed it and kept on past a sod house, a sort of dugout with one half below ground and the other half, the log and mud-caulked half, above ground. There was no smoke coming from the chimney, the door sagged inward on broken leather hinges and a broken old corral showed that no animals had been inside it for a long time.

" 'Be a hard land on homesteaders," said Emmett, eyeing that forlorn symbol of some man's grand dream gone sour. "You ever been inside one of those soddies?"

Matt shook his head, also looking across as they passed by. "Sure would be damp in wintertime, I'd think," he said. "Dank-damp is worse than wet-damp, for my money."

Now the northeastward mountains were little more than a blue blur against a curving horizon, but onward again, due eastward, another craggy range stood up off the world's far rim looking for all the world like crumpled cardboard.

"Gives a feller a sort of naked feelin', all this blamed open country. One thing you can say for Colorado, always plenty of mountains and hills." Emmett twisted, sniffed and tugged down his hatbrim to shade his eyes as he stared hard ahead. "You smell anything?" He asked, then didn't wait for Matt's reply. "I do. I smell a bottle of Old Overholt on a bar in a saloon dead ahead."

Matt smiled.

They saw the town an hour later without a shadow anywhere around because the sun was directly above them. There were a number of houses scattered at

21

random on the outskirts of the town, and some corrugated metal roofs shot shafts of rustily reflected light upwards and outwards. There wasn't a tree in sight, just this settlement dumped down in the middle of an endless prairie.

The grass got shorter and shorter until there wasn't much more than a green fuzz, the closer in they got. Here and there folks had staked out milk cows and saddlehorses. They even saw a little corral made of faggots confining six or eight woolly sheep. A light dust hung above the place as though its roadways were getting their share of wagons and riders. Coming in from the west as they were neither of them had had any idea what the town's name was because they hadn't used the stage road. But as they got among the farthest houses and met a boy with a big black dog, Emmett asked. The town's name, so the boy said, eyeing them both with lively curiosity, was Lodgepole. He also added that in case they didn't know where they were, this was Montana Territory.

They rode on through the crooked byway and eventually struck a roadway lined with residences which led them on to the main thoroughfare. Here, Lodgepole presented its opposing ranks of close-coupled buildings. There was even a bank, something very few cow towns had. And a big white-painted hotel in the center of town on the west side of the roadway. They eyed this structure as they rode past because it was both large and painted.

There were two liverybarns. One right across the road from the other. They chose the nearest one, turned in and got down. Between them they had thirty-seven dollars. Without any idea how long this might have to last they wouldn't go to the white-painted hotel, but

22

being horsemen they'd never stint where their animals were concerned. Still, as Emmett handed over one of his small reserve of silver dollars to the hostler, he gave the impression of a man parting from an old and very dear friend.

"Nice town," observed Matt, waiting and looking around.

Emmett ignored that to say, "You pay for the drinks, I paid for the horses."

They selected the most prosperous appearing saloon and headed for it. Cow town saloons were clearinghouses for information about what outfits were hiring, how much they paid, which had the best working conditions and whatever gossipy addenda might otherwise prove interesting to cowboys new to the land.

This particular saloon was made of old logs. It had obviously been something else before being turned into a saloon. "Army barracks," said Emmett. "Maybe an old-time tradin' post."

Matt nodded, uninterested. He jutted his chin across the road where a jailhouse stood with barred windows and a darkly uninviting but strongly functional facade. "Handy having the jail right across from the saloon. Save boot leather goin' and coming."

There were a number of cowboys in town. Some stood in little groups idly talking, some passed back and forth among the stores. These were all tophands. Ranches didn't keep any but the best men through the winter because aside from taking out jags of hay if and when the snow got too deep, there wasn't a whole lot to do. But rather than lose the best men, they were paid a reduced wage to hang around until spring broke again.

"I think I'm going to like it here," said Emmett, stooping a little as a bonneted woman went past, trying to peek up under the hood of the bonnet.

The saloon had no sign outside where nearly all saloons advertised their names, but inside over the back bar high up, a sign proclaimed in faded red letters that this was the *Kalispell House.* Emmett stumbled over that name three times before he phonetically sounded it out.

The room was large and musty. Smoke had been staining the log walls for a very long time. There was a big open space in front of the long bar and elsewhere there were wall benches—bolted down for safety's sake—as well as some two dozen poker tables. Although it was only slightly after noon, some of the tables had games going and along the bar a dozen or so men lounged, idly talking, killing time in out of the springtime heat, doing nothing and doing it splendidly as men can only do in a place where there are nothing but other men.

The barkeep was a short, pudgy man with a genial— and near blinding—smile, showing four gold teeth side by side in the front of his upper jaw. He was almost bald, had an old knife scar running up one side of his head where his hair had once covered it, and had the turned-up nose and bright blue eyes of an Irishman.

"What'll it be gents?" He inquired, missing very little as he waited, considering the long-legged pair of strangers.

"Two shots of Old Overholt," Matt stated, "and when you've got a minute, a little information."

The barman hopped away and scooped up two glasses with one hand, scooped up a partially filled bottle with the other hand and hopped back again. He was an old, old hand at this. "About work?" he said genially, pouring. "That'll be two bits for the whisky."

Matt made a little grimace. He hadn't quite reached his glass when that had been shot at him. He drew back the hand, dug for a quarter of a dollar, put it over in front of the barman and reached for the glass again.

"It's a mite early yet," stated the barkeep, gently frowning. "Nothing much doing for maybe another two, three weeks. Still, there is one outfit might could use a pair of good men."

Emmett said hopefully, "Yeah?"

"Yeah. The Farraday ranch. Two fellers quit out there, they tell me, a week back."

Emmett's face fell. He pushed forth his glass for a refill. "I don't think so," he told the barman almost mournfully. "We met Farraday this morning. Seems he don't like trespassers. Any other suggestions?"

The barman pursed his lips and thought, and before he spoke again he began to shake his head dolefully back and forth. "Like I said, it's too early yet, boys. Hang around for a week or two. Excuse me now, I got a customer."

4

THEY DIDN'T EAT UNTIL EARLY EVENING. POSTPONING the midday meal wasn't hard because they rarely had stopped on the trail to cook in the middle of the day anyway. And besides, they'd drunk up two dollars worth at the *Kalispell House* which, plus the cartwheel they'd handed the liverymen, left them a little shy of having thirty-four dollars left.

Down at the liverybarn, ordinarily another excellent source of job information, they got the same thing. "Try the Farraday ranch," the nighthawk told them. "Couple of the hands got fed up an' quit about a week ago."

This time though, instead of just mournfully shaking his head, Emmett said, "Why did they quit?"

The liveryman had nothing to do and felt loquacious. He was a nondescript individual with dull eyes and a loose, weak mouth. "Dunno exactly," he explained. "But I heard some of the other Farraday riders talkin' an' it seems Mike Thompson—that's Farraday's rangeboss—give 'em hell about not packin' their share of the load. So they upped and quit." The liveryman sucked his teeth and watched a pretty girl walk past out front; this was a purely reflex action. He was past sixty and running heavily to pure lard.

"That's a tough outfit," he said, speaking as though to himself more than to Emmett and Matt. "Old Farraday don't stand for no monkey business. He keeps near' a full crew year round."

"Kind of expensive," murmured Matt, gazing out into the well traveled roadway.

"He can afford it. Besides, he's always losin' beef." The liveryman hitched up his britches. They promptly sagged back down under the formidable out-thrust of his pulpy paunch. "Leastways that's what he's always claimin'. But no one else hereabouts says much about losing beef. Oh—now'n then some scruffy redskins carve up an old cow or two, but folks figure it's a sight cheaper to overlook this, than it is to make a big fuss an' maybe get the danged Injuns stirred up."

"Cheap rent," murmured Matt, watching a merchant across the road locking his roadside door.

The liveryman looked around. "What?"

"I said that's cheap rent," Matt repeated. Then he elaborated. "Let the Indians have a dozen or so old gummer cows a year for maybe ten or twenty thousand

26

acres of land."

The liveryman decided he didn't like the sound of that. He kept staring at Matt. Still, prudence was a splendid virtue, particularly since the longer the liveryman looked the more he read the signs aright about Matt Grady. Here was a powerfully muscled-up black-eyed big man with a jaw like granite. The liveryman made an easy compromise with his dislike of Matt's innuendo and sulkily said, "Yeah. Maybe it is cheap rent at that." Then he turned and went walking back down through the barn.

Afternoon faded fast once the sun dipped low. Shadows almost leapt out around the corners of buildings, down from the overhead rooflines and false fronts, some thick and abiding, some lean and greyly diluted.

There rose up now a soft scent of pine wood smoke in the pre-evening air. Supper fires were being stoked in three or four dozen kitchens. Lodgepole had satisfactorily completed another pleasant springtime day. Before many more went by summer would grace the land. By then the ranches would be hard at it gathering, marking, sorting, making up drives to rails end, doing all the interminable and unpredictable things which needed doing in cow country.

"Well," Emmett said with strong finality. "Let's go get some grub."

They crossed over to a hole-in-the-wall cafe, ordered meat and beans, coffee and apple pie, and ate. The place had its share of townsmen, a few hunters passing through from the eastward mountain range to the westward ranges, some Basques who were short, stocky men clannishly hanging together at a small table where they endlessly clacked in some outlandish tongue, and also a sprinkling of freighters and cattlemen. There was a strong hum of talk in this place which rolled over Matt and Emmett because none of the names mentioned meant anything and very little of the other talk held much significance either. Afterwards, they strolled back outside and rolled their smokes.

"Good beans," stated Matt, lighting up and holding the match for Emmett. "Good steak too—if a feller needed re-soling leather for his boots."

Emmett smiled and exhaled. There were lights coming on now, roundabout, visible down the byways in homes, also visible in the liverybarns, the saloons, and one of two of the main roadway stores which hadn't yet closed for the day. Emmett looked a little sadly at those lighted homes; the bad time of day for wanderers, ever, was evening. There were saucy-eyed women in those houses, and kids making a racket, and men padding around in their stockinged feet, smelling supper and feeling the deep-down satisfaction domestic men alone could feel. He dragged back a big breath of smoke and turned.

"Let's go up and maybe sit in a game," he said.

"What's the loss limit?" Matt inquired, turning to slowly pace along beside his pardner.

"Couple bucks. Say Matt; maybe we ought to take those hunters up on their offer. Go up and spend a few weeks around their lodges."

Matt walked along with his head lowered. "You can if you like, but I'll hang around Lodgepole."

Emmett said no more on this subject. They entered the saloon, which was now pulsing with sound and movement, went to the bar, squeezed in and flagged for drinks. The crowd was about equally divided between rangemen and townsmen. There wasn't a female in the place. A broad-shouldered man in a candy-striped shirt with sleeve garters was belting out a song at a piano which might not have been too bad, if anyone had been able to hear it.

The tables were full and men were loafing around them sipping their drinks, watching and waiting. From the looks of the pots where poker was being played it seemed that there was no immediate shortage of funds around the Lodgepole country.

"We'll be standin' here all night," Matt said. "Should've come up earlier."

Emmett lifted his eyebrows. "Who'd figure they start their games so early, in this country? Look at 'em; standin' around the tables like a bunch of hungry buzzards waitin' for a carcass to drop."

"There are other saloons," said Matt, setting his shotglass back upon the bar, empty.

" 'All be just like this one," rumbled Emmett, also moving away from the bar.

"Maybe not so crowded. Let's go."

They walked back out into the early night, no small feat in itself because of the crowded, buffeting tide of humanity they had to work their way through just to reach the doors, and afterwards, out upon the gloomy sidewalk where more people were pushing up to get inside.

They went northward a short distance and halted. Emmett removed his hat, reshaped the crown and dropped it back on to his head. "Where'n hell did they all come from?" He asked, genuinely interested. "We been around here most of the day an' there weren't near this many people abroad earlier."

"Come out at night," murmured Matt, "like a bunch of prairie owls—live in holes in the ground all day, hidin' from sunlight, then come popping out after dark."

They had been apart from mobs and uninhibited humanity too long. It didn't please them now to be jostled and poked and pushed left and right, so they remained slightly apart for a while, no longer so anxious to find a nice quiet game, because obviously, while there were plenty of games going in Lodgepole, they weren't quiet ones.

A sturdy, graying man with an open, amiable face and dead-level blue eyes came up, halted and nodded. "Evening, boys; what's the trouble—been on the trail so long all the noise and commotion bothers you?"

Emmett and Matt looked squarely around. Few men, indeed, could come up with so timely a syllepsis. There was a badge on this man's shirt front worn high, up above the breast pocket on the left side.

"Hit 'er right on the nail head, Sheriff," Emmett said, grinning. "Too long in quiet places."

The lawman pushed out his hand. "Frank Miller," he said, and made his assessment of transparent Emmett Ray, then shook with Matt Grady and was slower, more careful and probing in his appraisal here.

Emmett told Miller they'd just arrived in Lodgepole. He also told him why they were here. Sheriff Miller nodded, gazing southward where some riders were loping up the lamplight speckled roadway in a tight bunch. "It's a mite early yet for the outfits to be hiring," he said, dismissed the hurrying cowboys when they swerved in before the *Kalispell House,* and faced around again. "But there is one outfit that might—"

"Whoa," Matt said. "Not Farraday. Everyone suggests him. No good. We rode across his range today and he made it plenty plain he didn't like us for it."

Miller musingly regarded Matt. "I don't suppose you

made it easy for him," he said quietly.

Matt shrugged, turned and threw his black glance down the roadway saying nothing. Emmett stepped in to say, "Well; he was sort of pushin', Sheriff. Had four men with him an' got a little sassy with us."

"That's his way," said Sheriff Miller. "But I'll tell you boys; he's a mighty fair man to work for."

That brought Matt's attention back. "Yeah? Then how come a couple of men quit him last week?"

"I said Doc Farraday's a fair man," stated the law officer. "I *didn't* say anything about Mike Thompson, his rangeboss."

Emmett and Matt exchanged a look. "This rangeboss—is he swarthy-lookin' husky, mean-lookin' feller?"

Dave Miller made a faint smile. "I reckon that'd about describe him," he said. "But it'd depend a heap on how a feller felt towards Mike, how he looked to a man."

"That's how he looked to us," grunted Matt, remembering. "And Farraday was sittin' right there too, so we sort of got the notion they were birds of a feather."

"Well; maybe in some things they are. Farraday's been losing cattle for about a year now. Not just the usual few head beggin' Injuns rustle and eat; sometimes as many as twenty, thirty head at a clip. That's why he's suspicious of anyone crossin' his land."

Matt shrugged. Down the road a dancehall girl came out of one of the town's variety houses smoking a cigarette and gazing at the star-studded, bell-clear sky.

Emmett saw the girl too; she was something the hungers of lonely men revolved around; Doc Farraday, who was an unpleasant memory anyway, could fade into oblivion now.

Dave Miller saw the way they were watching the dancehall girl. "See you boys again," he murmured, smiled and strolled on. They lost him in the yonder crowd down by the *Kalispell House.*

Three cowboys entering town from the west cut across into the main roadway. Another band, about the same number, were walking their horses up from the southward range. The three riders saw the girl standing out there upon the edge of the plank walk and kept right on riding, but the other band, approaching from the south, when they saw her, turned in down there and tied up. She laughed at something one of them called softly to her from the tie rack. It was her laugh that broke the spell for Emmett and Matt; it was a high, harsh laugh without feeling or without humor. A mechanical laugh that grated on the nerves.

Emmett's disillusionment was quick and thorough. "Hell; let's get our blankets and bed down," he said, starting to turn.

Matt put out a hand. "Wait a second. Aren't those three tyin' up across the way the same fellers we met this morning on Farraday's range?"

Emmett turned to look. The riders were coming together across the road in front of a darkened small building, which was a harness shop but which didn't seem to interest them at all. They spoke among themselves, acting uncertain, acting troubled and anxious.

"It's them," answered Emmett. "Wonder what they're doin' here; come for a bottle maybe, or a fandango."

But Matt shook his head. "Something's bothering 'em. Watch."

The Sioux cowboys stood and sometimes shuffled

their feet, sometimes grunted words back and forth, but mostly they just stood.

"Out of cash," opined Emmett, but Matt shook his head again.

"Come on," he said, stepping down into roadway dust. They went over, were recognized, exchanged nods and waited. The one called Blackie was there. Braid was missing and one other buck; the three with Blackie were the younger men.

"We'll stand you fellers to a drink," Emmett said, smiling. "After all, you offered to share your meat with us."

Blackie shook his head. He studied Matt with morose eyes before turning towards Emmett to say, "No thanks. We come in to find the doctor. He's gone out of town. That leaves us in a fix."

"You got sickness?" Emmett asked.

One of the other men put a somber gaze upon Emmett. His face, dusky anyway, was hard to see where they were standing because of the deeper shadows from under an old wooden awning. "Yeh," he grunted. "You could say that. Sick kid at the camp. Got hurt today out huntin'."

"Well; what about your women? You must have someone up there who can—?"

"He needs sewin' up," stated Blackie. "Medicine men we got, but that's all a lot of bull. Oh, the herbs are good enough, but you know as well as I do when it comes to sewin' a man up . . ." Blackie shook his head.

Matt, studying their grave faces, said, "You goin' to stand around here wailin', or you goin' to find someone who can save the kid?"

One of the other rangemen turned on Matt, his hawkish, lean face showing anger, showing resentment.

33

"You talk big, cowboy," he said thinly. "Right now we need more'n big talk. Blackie told you—the sawbones is out of town."

Matt turned to fully face this man. "Then go on back," he snapped, "and do what's got to be done yourselves. If it's as bad as you say the kid'll likely die anyway—so what've got to lose? Doing anything is better than doing nothing!"

The angry Sioux kept staring. Under breath he said *"Dina sica."* No good. But this was his anger speaking because even as he said it, Matt's hard logic found support in the man's brain and his harsh expression altered. Finally, he looked around at Blackie, who was also considering Matt with a little irritation showing.

Blackie said, "You ever sew anyone up?"

Matt's baleful look atrophied. "Oh no," he growled, "you don't suck me into your troubles. I got enough of my own."

Emmett, though, cut in here to say, "Matt; how about old DeLancey's thoroughbred mare; you sewed her that time she rolled on a stump and gashed hell out of her flank. When it healed there wasn't even a hair-line scar."

The Indians were looking at Matt now as though in him lay their only salvation, or at least the salvation of the child back in their camp. Matt saw the looks and scowled darkly at his pardner.

"A horse is a horse," he snarled, "an' a kid is a human being."

"Nevertheless," exclaimed Emmett stoutly. "You just said yourself doin' something is better'n doing nothing. If these fellers never even sewed up a horse, then you've got that much more knowledge than they have. I'll go get the horses."

The men were watching for Matt's reaction. He glowered at Emmett, looked all around, said an oath under his breath and nodded. At once, Emmett walked away.

5

THEY LEFT LODGEPOLE, FIVE STRONG, AND RODE DUE west with the mealy old moon over their left shoulders until Blackie began to drift off northward a little where the first hills were dimly seen through paler shadows lying across the land. None of them said much until, about where Matt and Emmett had camped the night before, Blackie looked over at Matt.

"Farraday caught you. We watched. For a while it looked like trouble."

Matt shrugged, saying nothing.

They passed up towards the first gloomy belt of forest and Emmett suddenly sighted light far out and far southward. "A ranch," he said, surprised.

The man beside him nodded. "Yeah; Farraday's homeplace."

On up into the trees they went, Blackie leading, so dark it was like the inside of a well, yet the Sioux moved as sure-footedly as though they knew every tree, every break and rise and dip in these huge old ancient hills.

Emmett sniffed smoke a little after midnight, rolled his eyes around and caught his pardner's knowing nod. They were getting close.

The camp, when they first saw it, was down in a circular meadow perhaps a hundred acres in size. Trees stood as dark sentinels all around, the grass out there in the open was starshine colored, and a number of brush shelters were interspersed among some old dirty canvas tepees with their smoke-hole flaps raised on the north side to keep little gusts of springtime winds from filling them with smoke.

There were a number of fires burning low, turning to soft ash now because the day was gone, showing little more than winking scarlet coals among the embers, but the moment all five riders appeared out of the forest darkness, shod hooves striking stone outcroppings on the steep descent into that hidden big meadow, shadows rose up off the ground to stand stoically watching. It looked to Emmett and Matt as though there had to be about thirty people gathered here in this pot-hunters' camp. One of the riders veered off. Another also left them. By the time they got to the last teepee only Blackie remained. He swung down, tossed his reins to a stripling youth naked to the waist, motioned for Matt and Emmett to do likewise, then bent to catch hold of the door flap and hold it back.

Inside, in the exact center of the teepee, an oak fire burnt with a steady, hot blue flame without making any sound at all. There was a withered, ugly old woman in there crooning and gently rocking forth and back. She didn't see the newcomers. Her rheumy old dark eyes were fixed upon some distant point only she knew of, but her crooning rose and fell, rose and fell, making an off-key, monotonous dirge that seeped deep into everything, even into the hearts of the men.

A handsome light-skinned woman glanced up at Blackie, at Matt and Emmett. She considered Emmett longest, and if ever a man saw a silent scream for help in a woman's eyes, Emmett saw it in that woman's face. She obviously thought that fair-haired Emmett was the doctor. Beside her on a pile of skins and trade blankets lay a coppery boy not yet in his teens with a soggy red-stained cloth wrapped around his left side.

Matt went across and knelt. The boy was rational. In the bluish light of the teepee fire he eyed Matt with a black and glittering stare. Emmett, dropping to one knee beside Matt, whispered, "Fever; he's burnin' up with it."

Matt didn't answer. He eased back the bandage, bent and looked, straightened around and irritably said to the woman. "You got a lamp or a candle?"

It was Blackie who moved. He ducked low and left the teepee. He returned within minutes holding aloft a hissing coal oil lamp that had to be turned down because it was too bright. He stood back there holding the lamp, his face expressionless. Behind him silent people crowded inside. The only sound was their slow breathing. The only other sound was the old grandmother rocking gently and making her endless death prayer. Emmett thought he heard a soft-sighed whisper among those still people: "Crow."

Matt, if he heard that, gave no sign of it. He turned and gestured for the pot of water at the end of the fire. It was brought over and set close. He dipped his hands in, made a grimace at Emmett because the water was scalding hot, then went to work removing the crude bandage.

Emmett swallowed painfully. The slash was just below the lad's lowest rib. It was deep and ragged and badly swollen: was darker by far than the boy's naturally dark hide. He didn't like the looks of that wound so he raised his eyes and found the boy watching him. Emmett smiled. The boy's eyes lit up a little but otherwise his face didn't change.

"You got a sewing needle?" Matt asked the woman, without looking at her, as he bathed the wound and picked lint out of it. "Buckskin makes better bandages, no frayed ends get stuck . . . Well; where's the needle and some gut to sew with?" He demanded irritably, turning at last to stare at the woman. She looked up. Blackie nodded, still holding the hissing lamp in his rigid arm. She rose and went scuttling across the teepee.

Matt leaned back, gazed at Emmett, gazed all around at the still, empty faces and finally put his stare upon Blackie. "How did this happen?" He asked, speaking quietly, as though some incredible suspicion was in his mind which he was having difficulty believing. "No animal clawed the kid; that's what you told me."

"No," averred Blackie. "I said he was out hunting. I didn't say an animal got him."

The woman returned, bent and handed Matt a needle threaded with the kind of very fine sinew used to string beads on. He took it and kept looking upwards. "Well; do you know how it happened, Blackie?"

"I know. Right now you sew him up. Talk later."

Emmett nudged Matt and leaned over a little. "You better put cold water on it, otherwise the damned swellin'll increase and bust out the stitches."

Matt looked down, frowning. "No. It's already as swollen as it'll get. Be better to sew it up now. Got to clean it first though. Em; set another kettle to heat. And Em—shut up that cussed old woman; she makes my nerves crawl."

Emmett got up and slowly turned. Blackie was shaking his head at him. Emmett understood. Old Grandmother belonged to another time; everything they were about to do was foreign to her. Even Blackie and his cowboy friends were alien to her. But they

38

understood her if she understood them or not. Emmett went after more water and another iron kettle. A squat, very dark woman went out with him to help.

It was a long night.

The hurt lad's face got shiny with sweat but otherwise he showed nothing as Matt worked on him. There were grey circles under his eyes and a faint but noticeable white ridge above his upper lip. Emmett took his hand and held it. This brought a small spark to the lad's eyes, but otherwise they were grave in his childlike face, struggling hard to summon the dignity which was required to meet this grueling test.

Emmett, who had seen his share of raw violence, was an unwilling spectator here. The heat was a steady force which carried with it gamey odors and a powerful drowsiness.

Suddenly, the old grandmother's chant ceased. She stopped her gentle rocking as well, but her eyes were still fixed in that trance-like stare upon something far distant no one else could see.

Matt leaned back. Sweat dripped from his nose and chin. He flung it off. The boy's face softened, his eyes closed, his grip on Emmett's hand slackened. A low, sad sigh passed among the people. Blackie, still holding the lamp outright in his rigid arm, looked from where Emmett sat, like some imagined dark demon, stalwart and impassive, out of a bad dream. Blackie slowly lowered his arm.

Emmett got stiffly to his feet, made his way outside where the eastward sky was going pale now, turning back the darkness of the night with a slow, inexorable force, and felt a cool pre-dawn breeze brush lightly across his face.

Overhead a million stars looked down where velvet

night still lived, but this night was ended, and in its ending was a promise of new day—new life. Someone came out and hurried away. Others also departed. Finally, one of the men they'd ridden up here with from Lodgepole, came over and held out a bottle. Emmett took it, tilted it, took three fiery swallows and passed it back. Hot tears burnt unshed in his eyes. He dashed them away with his knuckles.

Blackie and Emmett came out. Inside, old grandmother went back to her keening song again. The man with the bottle passed it around. No one said anything. Here, in the chill early dawn, trails divided. The dead went one way, the living another way. No man could know any more about one trail than he could about the other trail, and yet, in the steadily brightening steely heavens was the promise that whenever a man died—wherever he died—the race of man would not only survive, it would ultimately triumph.

"The woman will give you a horse," said Blackie quietly.

Matt, gazing at his toes, said in a voice as bitter as ashes, "Why? He died didn't he?"

"Because you did what you could."

"She can keep the damned horse." Matt would have said more but Emmett, as always, headed off unpleasantness. He knew the look and the mood of his pardner.

"How did it happen?" He asked.

The man with his bottle shook it, found there was still some left and threw back his head to drink. Another shadowy silhouette joined them as silent as a mist, in front of the canvas teepee with its door flap closed, shutting some in and shutting others out.

Matt said: "You heard him—he asked how it

40

happened." But before Blackie replied Matt also said, "Make it good, pardner, because I know a bullet slash when I see one."

The whisky drinking man hiccupped. One of the others turned and softly walked away. Over in front of a ragged brush shelter someone tossed wood on a dying fire and tiny sparks jumped wildly into the night. People moved here and there because another day was strengthening and hunters knew the best times to get meat—coming out of their grassy beds deer were easy targets. Grouse huddling drowsily close on low limbs were ready to be killed—this held true also at sunset. The best times to kill for meat—sunup, sunset.

"He went hunting with another boy," said Blackie. "They wounded a doe and chased her out of the forest. She was fat, they said, and they were kids with their first good kill. You know."

Emmett was beginning to get the drift of this. He very gradually straightened up to his full height, feeling the first pangs of shock, of a gut-shot-like illness.

"It was an hour after Farraday had stopped you, out there. They were heading back for the home place. The boys were after their doe. They didn't see the men; didn't ever hear them. That one inside the teepee—the dead boy—he raised up out of the grass to shoot the doe where she faltered—and one of them cut loose."

"Farraday. . . ?" Said Emmett, incredulous.

"One of them. Maybe Farraday, maybe one of the others."

"But. But good lord, he's only a kid—ten or twelve . . ."

Matt stirred, raised his brooding eyes to the steely east and blew out a ragged breath. "What you figure to do?" He asked Blackie, dropping his gaze to consider the faces around him.

Blackie said nothing. None of them spoke. Another man turned softly and silently paced away. The last one to do this was the man with the empty bottle clutched in his fist. There were only the three of them left. Emmett squeezed his eyes tight closed then sprang them wide open again; it helped visibility.

"The law says we got no right out there on Farraday's land," stated Blackie in a dull tone, after an interval of long silence had passed. "If we go huntin' the man who shot him—and shoot him—you know what'll happen, Matt?"

Emmett looked at his pardner but Matt didn't speak. He clearly wasn't going to speak. He had that closed-down expression on his face Emmett had seen before, which meant Matt was far away in a black jungle of private thoughts.

The old woman's moaning went on and on. The sky steadily brightened. Hunters strode forth to catch their horses out across the meadow, where dew shone with magic colors. Women worked stoically over the breakfast fires. Children, subdued now, moved listlessly around the camp, not quite comprehending yet aware that in the night some blight had settled upon their elders.

Matt said in a strangling voice, "Let's get out of here, Em. Where the hell are the horses?"

Blackie didn't move to go with them, but remained by the teepee, his eyes dull, his face impassive. As the sunlight strengthened it struck across the crude painting above him on the dirty canvas. Someone had made a sketch symbolic of the owner's name above the door flap. A black cloud.

When they found their animals and untied them, turned them a couple of times to ease the stiffness from night-long standing, Matt leaned across his saddle seat looking back.

"Was he shootin' close to scare 'em or was he tryin' to hit the kid?" He asked, not particularly speaking to Emmett, then he swung up over leather, gathered his reins and turned. They rode down through the quiet camp and out of it back the way they'd come. Emmett had nothing to say. He was relieved though, to be out of there. Not just because of what had happened, but because he knew what those people would do now—the old ones anyway: Blacken their faces and, among the women at least, gash their flesh, perhaps slit an ear or cut off a finger. Crow, Piegan, Lakota or Dahkota, it was pretty much the same when death came to strike down a loved one.

They were heading back down through the trees, their saddles tilting up behind as the land ran on down country towards Doc Farraday's ocean of swaying springtime grass, when Matt twisted to look backwards.

"No one's that lousy a shot," he exclaimed. "If you wanted to scare a kid you wouldn't shoot close—you wouldn't have to. But if you aim to hit him, an' he was movin', that's about how the wound would look."

Emmett had shrewdly come to this identical conclusion some time before, so he rode along now without saying a word.

6

BY THE TIME THEY GOT BACK TO LODGEPOLE THE SUN was well up, people were busily abroad, and down at the liverybarn there was a thinner man on duty to take their animals.

43

"I need a drink," Emmett said, and struck out for the *Kalispell House* without even waiting to ascertain whether or not Matt was following. He was; they went through the batwing doors almost side by side and the daytime barkeep looked a little surprised. Most men had just finished breakfast.

"Two shots of Old Overholt," said Emmett, planking down the silver in advance. The liquor came, went down like molten fire and the barman held the bottle poised until Emmett nodded, gasping, then reached for his second one.

"You fellers got a thirst early," murmured the barkeep. "Don't usually peddle much hard liquor so early in the day."

Matt's black eyes lifted. "You object?" He asked.

The barman's eyes widened. "Not at all," he said quickly. "Not at all." He put down the bottle, turned and walked away.

Somewhere outside and southward a man was banging upon an anvil; it made a pleasant, almost musical sound. Northward a dog was excitedly barking. There was a faint and diminishing scent of cook stove wood smoke hanging in the atmosphere. Two boys went by out in the roadway driving wooden hoops ahead of them and laughing.

"Damn," muttered Emmett, turning his back to the bar, hooking his elbows behind himself. "Makes a feller's hide crawl. Fifteen, sixteen miles from here folks are gashin' their flesh and wailing their hearts out. Down here—nothing's changed one little bit."

"Like being in two worlds at the same time, Em," Matt muttered. "Like havin' one foot in yesterday and one foot in today."

Emmett vigorously nodded. "That's it exactly, Matt.

44

That's exactly it, by golly. You want another shot?"

"No. Two's enough. Besides, all I really wanted was to sort things out a little in my head."

"Then let's go get some breakfast. I'm feelin' better now."

Outside, the roadway was brisk with traffic, foot traffic, horseback traffic, and wagon traffic. Everything looked the same as it had the day before, and that also helped. For Emmett at least, it had to be this way. The eerie sensation of being part of two entirely different worlds, an ancient one and a modern one, had almost been too shattering.

"Morning, boys," a boomingly pleasant deep voice said, as they turned into that same hole-in-the-wall cafe where they'd previously eaten. It was Sheriff Dave Miller holding open the door for them and standing clear, his genial features calm and poised and as they'd been before, watchful but not troublesome. "Sort of late gettin' breakfast, aren't you?"

Emmett stepped through, smiled and slowed to a dragging halt. Behind him, Matt would have pushed on across to the corner except that Emmett blocked this for him.

"Sheriff," said Emmett, "you get many murders around the Lodgepole country?"

Miller, stopped in his tracks by the bluntness of this, ceased smiling. "Not many," he replied, gazing hard at Emmett. "Hasn't been a genuine murder in a long time. A few gun fights, but no murders."

"One more question, then," stated Emmett, conscious of Matt's dark scowl in his direction. "If a feller killed someone and no one ever turned him in for it, d'you reckon it'd eat on him until he did talk about it?"

Miller's blue stare turned hard and thoughtful as he

45

slowly answered that question. "If you're still talkin' about murder, cowboy, I'd say the answer was—no. Because a murderer's got no heart or feelings to start with, otherwise he wouldn't be a murderer. You follow me?"

Matt plucked at Emmett's sleeve and growled, "Come on. Let's get some grub. What kind of damfool talk is this, anyway?"

Emmett responded to the plucking, but as he turned away he said, "Thanks, Sheriff; I just wondered. Nothin' to it but my curiosity." He went on across the room with Matt and got astraddle the counter bench, but back by the doorway Dave Miller didn't depart at once; he stood gazing across at Emmett's back.

Matt ordered for them both and turned with an angry growl. "What're you tryin' to do—stir up the law?"

Emmett shook his head and glanced right and left along the counter. There were a few other late-eaters, perhaps seven or eight, but none were closer than ten feet. "No, I wasn't even thinkin' of the law, Matt, what I was wondering was whether Farraday would care enough about that shootin' yesterday to try an' find out whether anyone got hurt or not."

"Well, don't ask that damned lawman, you idiot, because now he'll get to wondering too—not about Farraday but about you'n me."

"Someone ought to tell him, Matt. I don't care how big Farraday is, he shouldn't be bigger'n the law. That kid died; someone ought to have to pay for that."

"Keep out of it," stated Matt, as their meal came. "It's done and finished with."

Emmett slowly turned to scan his pardner's features. This was a quite new Matthew Grady to him. He'd seen Matt get involved in his share of fights over the past few

46

years, and never once before had he heard Matt make such a statement as he'd just made. In fact, it was usually the other way around—Emmett was the one who took the disentangling view.

Matt looked up from his plate, caught his pardner's expression and defensively said, "Well; at least for now let it go. I got something in mind."

Emmett's expression altered, he turned and lit into his food. Now, things were back to normal, and normal, in this case, he had a dark feeling, wasn't going to be the same as normal in any other mess they gotten themselves embroiled in.

After eating they strolled over to the liverybarn to check on their horses, and after that, as they stepped out of the aromatic liverybarn runway, they encountered the sheriff again, but this time though, the meeting was clearly not by accident as it had been over at the cafe, no matter how casual Miller had contrived to make it seem.

"Feel better with some grub under your belts?" The lawman genially asked, and fooled neither Emmett or Matt by his casual approach.

"Some better," said Emmett, shying away from further talk with Miller.

"Where'd you boys bed down last night?" The lawman asked.

Matt made a big all-encompassing gesture as he said, "Out a ways. Can't spare the price for a hotel room. Don't much care for them anyway."

"Is that a fact?" Stated Miller, his gaze turning a little hard, a little suspicious. "Do you always ride out a ways an' bed down like that?" He waved a hand towards the interior of the barn. "The nighthawk said you two rode out about nine o'clock last night."

Matt's cheeks darkened, his eyes turned stone black. "You checkin' on us, Sheriff? Because if you are, forget it. We're not wanted anywhere."

"You wouldn't have to be wanted. All you'd have to have is some information the law ought to know about. Like murder, for example."

"Oh hell," grunted Matt. "Em was just askin' one of his usual damfool questions. He's like that." Matt turned on Emmett. "I told you someday you'd land in a peck of trouble with your flappin' mouth."

Sheriff Miller was stumped again exactly as he'd been stumped over at the cafe, so when Matt jerked his head angrily at Emmett and the pair of them hiked away, he said nothing to further detain them. Still, after watching them head across towards the *Kalispell House Saloon,* he went gravely along towards his jailhouse where he had stacks of wanted posters.

Matt bought two beers at the bar inside the saloon, got a deck of cards and went across to a table with Emmett in tow. As he got settled for a game of two-handed stud poker he looked balefully from beneath his hatbrim, but he didn't say anything, he just cut the cards and started dealing. He was still angry. Emmett didn't say anything either.

They played for two hours stopping once while Emmett returned to the bar for refills, and stopping once more when three dusty cowboys came noisily inside in the late afternoon to hoist a few before getting on back to the ranch.

The winnings traded hands a number of times. This was an old contest between these two. This was, in fact, how they'd initially come together; neither could quite triumph over the other at poker, both felt the other was really an inferior player, and this off-and-on competition

48

had taken them all over the ranges of Colorado and Wyoming, and now up into Montana as well, still without its basic issue being resolved.

The three cowboys stamped out of the saloon as noisily as they'd entered it. Later, with shadows falling, men began drifting in, one and two at a time, but later on, after suppertime when dusk was well settled upon the land, patrons began trooping in, in greater numbers. Once, Emmett suggested they take their game of two-handed somewhere else because it didn't strike him as being fair for just the pair of them to tie up a table when otherwise six players could get a game going. Matt shook his head and scooped in a pot. Occasionally a cowboy would drift over and ask about buying in. Matt would do the same thing—shake his head. It didn't occur to Emmett that Matt was deliberately acting like this until, near eight o'clock, a number of booted, spurred range riders walked in out of the yonder night, and Emmett instantly recognized Doc Farraday's rangeboss, swarthy and mean-eyed Mike Thompson. Then it struck Emmett just under the heart what Matt was up to.

He looked at the men with Mike Thompson, recognized two as having been among the riders with Farraday and Thompson the morning of the day before, and thought another two looked vaguely familiar also. He straightened up in his chair, placed his cards face down atop the table and waited for Matt's black, glittering gaze to drift back to him from the bar where Matt had been steadily regarding Thompson and the other Farraday riders.

"You better forget it," Emmett advised softly. "At least until the odds are better."

Matt considered his cards, discarded one and dealt

himself a replacement as he said, "Em; the odds'll never be any better. Haven't you figured that out yet? Farraday's men got few enough friends; they don't go around singly." Matt folded his cards and tossed them down. He looked steadily at his pardner. "You want some fresh air?" He asked. "Seems to me it's gettin' to smell bad in here."

Emmett rose, not the least cognizant of whatever it was Matt had in mind, but willing enough to leave this place. Matt was primed and yeasty. If they stayed longer there was going to be a bad fight. Outside at least, they'd be clear of Thompson and the other Farraday riders. "Let's go," be said.

Matt walked out first, Emmett followed. Behind them, several range riders crossed quickly to stake a claim on their abandoned table.

Outside, the air was soft-scented and clean, the skies shone with an unearthly pewter light, young lovers strolled hand in hand and older people, shy most of youth's illusions, paced blandly along simply content to be enjoying themselves after a day of toil.

Matt rolled a smoke and passed Emmett the sack. They both lit up off the same match, then stood in their own little private tobacco cloud for a time saying nothing.

"Em," said Matt, after a while, his black gaze soberly set upon the distant black hulking peaks visible only because they were darker than the sky around them, "you remember that fight we had down in Denver that time with all those bully boys?"

Emmett nodded. He remembered. He had held the others under his gun while Matt had squared off with the biggest, loudest, of the city toughs. It had been a fight to make history.

"Yeah, I remember."

"Well; what say? They'll be comin' out of there sooner or later."

"Why, Matt? You say yourself the kid's dead."

"I want to know which one did it. It's the only way they'll talk. I'll start with Thompson. All right?"

Emmett inhaled, exhaled. "All right. But afterwards, what?"

"*Then* we'll bring in your friend the sheriff. But first I want to break someone up for that. You understand?"

"Yeah I understand. It could be a long wait."

Matt shrugged and went silent. He had the patience.

7

DAVE MILLER, OUT MAKING HIS NIGHTTIME ROUNDS, stopped to talk a little. Dave's attitude was different. He'd made his search through the wanted flyers and had come up with nothing. This of course did not mean Emmett and Matt couldn't be wanted somewhere or weren't outlaws, but it did mean they weren't notorious ones, otherwise someone, somewhere, would have put out posters on them. But Dave Miller was as tolerant as most frontier lawmen were or became, if they lived long enough, and on top of that Dave, at forty-three, realized that not everyone was so virtuous that they had not at one time or another run afoul of the law. The only pristine people in this world were the drones; the ones who never ran a risk or took a chance; the dull, humdrum, unimaginative people.

"Talked to a small cowman from south of town today," he said, unaware that his presence had turned both Emmett and Matt warily uncomfortable. "He said

51

he could use one man for a few days, if that'd help you fellers out any."

Matt, leaning in dark shadows, said nothing and scarcely even glanced around, which was oftentimes his way, but Emmett, more sensitive to the feelings of others, smiled at Sheriff Miller as he explained that they didn't want to break up.

"Anyway, we'll hang an' rattle until the big outfits commence hiring. We can make it, I reckon."

Miller shrugged. "It was just a thought. Sure a fine night, isn't it?"

"Sure is," agreed Emmett, without much enthusiasm.

Noise from within the saloon at their backs rose into a raucous bedlam. Miller looked around and back again. "Must be a bunch of rangemen inside," he guessed. "They sure let their hair down when they hit Lodgepole. Well; it's been a long enough winter. Feller can't blame 'em too much."

"No," agreed Emmett, "a feller sure can't."

"See you fellers again. Good night."

"Yeah," breathed Emmett in relief. "Good night, Sheriff."

They turned their heads to watch Sheriff Miller walk on southward, his heavy shoulders and chest giving his walking gait a slight roll as he progressed through the patches of light and dark.

"Thought he was going to sit down an unroll his bed-roll," muttered Emmett. "Whew!"

They went on with their endless waiting. Matt finally said, "Hell; don't they go from one saloon to another like most rangemen do? What's so wonderful about the *Kalispell House* a feller'd want to stay in there half the night without moving?"

Emmett had no idea. "Where you reckon it got such a

tongue twistin' name?" He repeated it. "Kalispell House: Sounds more like a hotel than a saloon."

"Not Sioux," said Matt. "A lot of the other names in this country are Sioux, but that one sure isn't."

A short man stepped out of the saloon, reached up to resettle the hat atop his head, square his shoulders and carefully set his course for another saloon diagonally across the road. He stepped down and started ahead, walking with the rigidly controlled effort of a drunk who didn't wish to appear drunk.

Someone inside began banging out a tune named *Lorena* on the piano. Normally, *Lorena* was a poignant song, but the way it was now being mangled it was scarcely recognizable as the same song at all, and that was even before some frog-voiced cowboy decided to treat the world to the benefits of his singing ability. After that, even the off-key piano sounded good. Emmett dolefully shook his head. A man didn't realize just how ridiculous he himself was, in his cups, until, stone sober, he listened to others who'd had a mite too much panther sweat under the belts.

Two older men came out of the *Kalispell House*. Both were big, rawboned old men, and both probably had as big a load as the men they'd just left behind, but neither of them showed it as they rolled along southward sober as a pair of owls.

Emmett was standing with his shoulders to the front, outer wall of the saloon. He was layered over by dense shadows. Unless passersby looked closely they scarcely saw him at all. Matt, on the other hand, was at the front edge of the walkway slouched against one of the spaced poles which held aloft the wooden overhang. He had his back to the saloon's doors and didn't bother to turn when departing patrons left the place. It was Emmett who would glance at each entering or leaving customer, so it was Emmett, when several men came stamping out into the gloomy night, who cleared his throat, bringing Matt up off his post in a loose, casual turn.

There were four or five of these cattlemen leaving the building. It was difficult to say how many because they had to crowd through the bat-wing doors all in a bunch. Furthermore it was dark. Matt singled one of those men out, though. Emmett saw him do this; saw Matt start moving. Emmett stepped sideways five feet, lowered his right hand, raised it, and pushed blue steel into the nearest cowboy's ribs.

"Hey Mike," Matt said, drawing Thompson's attention loosely around by the sharpness, the strong menace, in that soft call. Thompson's face was darkly flushed, his swarthiness glistened with sweat and his eyes were darkly bright and bold.

"Step out here, Mike."

Thompson did not recognize Matt but he took a step forward, and as he did that Emmett got between Mike and the others so they could see his six-gun. "Relax," Emmett said. "Just stand easy boys, and you'll see a little action. Make any wrong moves an' you'll never live to see who walks away from this."

The Farraday ranch hands suddenly became sober. They gazed dumbly from Emmett's .45 to his face. If they recognized him none of them gave any indication of it. None of them seemed to grasp what was happening; none of them went for his gun. It had all happened too smoothly, too surprisingly. Emmett gestured for them to step away from the saloon doorway, which they mechanically did.

"Mike, I'm goin' to ask you a question," said Matt, from the sidewalk's edge. "How you answer it is goin'

54

to decide how you leave town tonight—flat-out or straight-up."

Thompson's loose grin was gone but he still did not appear to catch the drift of all this. "Hell," he said, "I know you now. You're that feller we run off the range yesterday morning."

"Yeah," murmured Matt. "But that's not what's stuck in my craw today, Mike. After you ran us off you fellers rode on saw a kid hunting and one of you shot him. What I want to know is: Which one of you fired that shot?"

Thompson stood gazing at Matt for a while before he spoke again. He was putting loose ends together and arriving at his decision. "Go to hell," he said, and stepped back. Mike was also sober now. In stepping back he'd indicated what he meant to do—get enough room to gunfight.

Matt made a wry face at him. "That's no good, Mike. Look over your shoulder. There's a .45 on your back. Go for your gun now, and you'll never get it out of leather. Once more—who fired that shot?"

Mike licked his lips. He didn't turn to see Emmett back there; he didn't have to, his friends were being too still and quiet. He knew perfectly well they were under a gun, otherwise they'd be joining in this quiet but lethal exchange.

He made another decision; actually, it was an adjustment to altered circumstances. He was a brawny, confident man scarred by rough experiences, his life had been hard and tawny, he didn't scare easily and what he saw before him now was a feisty range rider much like dozens of other feisty rangemen he'd faced before.

"What's it to you?" He demanded, letting his body turn loose, letting his right arm come clear of his holstered pistol, getting set for what was going to happen and stalling a little while he got set.

"The kid died," said Matt. "That's what it is to me. What kind of man shoots ten-year-old kids?"

"A trespasser is a trespasser, cowboy."

"Yeah? An' Farraday shoots 'em? Then what happened to his guts when he had my pardner an' me under his thumb yesterday?"

"Don't you never worry about Doc Farraday's guts," snarled Thompson, standing hard down in his boots, even-balanced and ready now. "Just worry about your own!"

Matt put his head slightly to one side. He knew what was passing through the other man's head; Thompson would make his move any second now. Behind them several unobservant patrons left the saloon and walked on past unaware of anything save perhaps the lateness of the hour. Across the road two cowboys at a tie rack were jawing at each other over some pettiness, their voices sounding full of small meanness, garrulous irritation.

"Once again, Mike: Who shot the kid?"

"You're a stranger hereabouts," said Thompson, masking his intentions with words. "You've just stuck your neck out a country mile, cowboy, buttin' in where you got no . . ." Thompson launched himself straight at Matt. It had been a good enough ruse, except for the fact that Matt had been expecting it. He stepped lightly to one side, let Mike lunge in close, and struck him a sledging blow in the side that impeded Thompson's direction but not his impetus. Thompson staggered on off the sidewalk and stumbled ahead through roadway dust, caught himself and turned, ten feet away.

Matt stepped out into the roadway also. Across the

56

way in front of Dave Miller's jailhouse those two jangling cowboys abruptly fell silent as they stood ready to mount up. Finally one of them said, startled. "Hey Jack—look yonder. A damned fight." His pardner, with one foot in the stirrup, stepped away from his horse to turn and watch. "Be damned if it ain't," he said.

"Better answer," grated Matt, stalking his man. "Better save yourself a beatin', Mike."

Thompson's eyes were wide open; he'd been not only beaten to the punch, he'd also been hurt. Everything he'd learned in other encounters like this suddenly made him cautious. He'd been beaten before; he wasn't invincible. But also, he'd come out top dog just often enough to make him want to believe Matt's speed and power, at least for now, had been a combination of fortunate accidents in his adversary's favor. But, as Matt came on, Thompson moved away. He sidled around, both fists cocked, his eyes like black stones, wary and watchful and wanting very much to batter Matt to the ground.

"You goin' to tell me?" Matt asked, twisting as Thompson worked around to get him off balance.

"I'll tell you," Thompson said in a whisper. "When you're knocked out, I'll whisper it in your ear."

Matt stepped away, stepped in and flicked a little jab that made Thompson roll his head sideways. The second he had Farraday's rangeboss on the defensive, Matt dropped low and jumped in swinging a combination of blows to Thompson's middle. Both connected. Thompson's breath broke out in a grunt. He ran backwards and sprang sideways again, once more forcing Matt to pause long enough to untrack his feet and turn. As before, this was Thompson's opportunity to attack, but also as before, Thompson didn't, because

57

he'd been hit hard and hurt.

"Fight," growled Matt. "Never mind that fancy footwork—fight!"

Thompson stopped moving. He had an acidly bitter taste in his throat from those blasting mid-riff punches. He was being standoffish now. It was abundantly clear that if Matt's initial success on the sidewalk had perhaps been accidental, this time no combination of circumstances had helped him. Thompson began sidling again, his fists still cocked.

Matt straightened up, put both hands on his hips and glared, his face made ugly by its powerfully scornful expression. He didn't say anything, he just kept turning to face Thompson, leaving himself wide open to the other man's attack. But again Thompson missed his chance.

"Hell," Matt growled in deep contempt. He started after Thompson. Over across the road those two cowboys were standing like carved statues. Behind them on both sides were other men, surprised to witness this fight because there wasn't a sound being made as the two battlers maneuvered. Usually, brawls such as this one had supporters who roared encouragement. Usually too, there were friends of both men who would jump in to take sides. Not this time.

Matt got Thompson backing towards the saloon, his intention to catch Mike as his ankles struck the wood planking back there. But Thompson anticipated this and suddenly got clear. He then made another of those quick, devastating lunges of his, and this time he was at least partially successful. Matt rocked back to let a fist graze his cheek and push on up into his hair knocking his hat ten feet out into the dark dust. He stepped rapidly sideways and Thompson went past clean. Matt was too far off to hit him as he'd done before. Thompson turned and evidently without really thinking, tried it again. This time he'd made the worst blunder possible, because Matt was solidly set, thick legs planted wide, body hunched forward, both fists up and waiting; this time Matt wasn't going to yield an inch.

They came together with a shock every spectator winced from, even Emmett, over there behind his captives, gasped. Thompson was rocked by impact, so was Matt, but he was at least prepared. He hit Thompson in the middle, clubbed him over the heart, fired a slashing blow higher that made the rangeboss's head snap back violently, then as Thompson staggered and half turned as though to spring clear, Matt hit him a stunning blow under the ear.

Thompson's arms dropped, his shoulders sagged, his solid legs turned loose at the knees and folded. Thompson fell in a heap at Matt's feet. Except for that man inside the saloon beating upon the piano, the roadway was deathly still until Emmett pushed his gun into one of the other men's back and said, "All right, cowboy; you're next. I'm going to feed you into the chopper one at a time until we get an answer."

"Hold it," the cowboy said thinly in a fading tone. "Not me, mister. I ain't that good a fighter. I'll tell you who fired that shot—you're lookin' at him right now lyin' out there in the roadway. It was Mike. But he didn't mean to kill nobody."

8

"THEY NEVER DO," SAID A DRY VOICE IN THE northward night. Dave Miller strode ahead, pushed past some stunned bystanders and tapped Emmett on the shoulder. "Put up that gun, cowboy." Emmett obeyed, uncertain though about what was now going to happen. The harder he tried to read Sheriff Miller's face in the gloom the more uncertain he got, too, because Miller didn't look the least bit perturbed. He stepped off the plankwalk, strolled out to join several other bystanders in gazing at beaten Mike Thompson, and lifted his stare to Matt.

"No one," he quietly said, "gets preoccupied about murder, cowboy, unless he's got a reason. That goes for your pardner as well as anyone else."

Matt said nothing. He was wrapping the bloody knuckles of his left hand with his soiled handkerchief. Miller noticed and asked if he needed a doctor. Matt shook his head and prodded Thompson with a boot toe.

"Not me. But maybe he does. I hit him in the middle and skinned some knuckles on his gun belt buckle."

"He'll be all right," mused Sheriff Miller, none too concerned. "Couple of you fellers drag him out of the road, though. Never can tell in the dark when someone might ride over him." Miller jerked his head at Matt. "Come on over to my office," he said, then turned and repeated that order louder in Emmett's direction. Afterwards, when Emmett moved around the other Farraday riders, Miller said to them, "Get Mike on a horse and take him home. Tell Mister Farraday I'll be out to see him tomorrow."

There still wasn't much of a crowd around. The fight hadn't lasted long enough to draw much of one. But now, as they began drifting off, the spectators gave Matt and Emmett glances of vast respect and sharp interest.

"You ought to lock him up," said Matt, gazing at Thompson's star-washed, still and battered face at his feet. "Didn't you hear what his friend said? You let him leave town an' you'll likely never see him again."

Miller ignored this and jerked his head as he led the way to his office. That man at the *Kalispell House* was still blissfully unaware of anything happening outside as he belabored his piano. The last of the bystanders drifted off. Thompson's friends went out to get him clear of roadway traffic. Matt shrugged at Emmett and the pair of them followed Sheriff Miller into his lighted little cubbyhole of a cluttered office, which smelt strongly of horse sweat, man sweat, and pipe tobacco.

Miller motioned towards a bench, waited until Matt and Emmett were seated, then in the same imperturbable, quiet manner, said, "All right; Mike shot someone: Who?"

Emmett might have spoken but Matt shook his head at the sheriff. "Forget it. It's a sort of private affair."

Miller gazed from Matt to Emmett, his gaze thoughtfully assessing. "How about it, Mister Ray—you figure murder's a private affair."

"Well . . . I reckon I'll go along with my pardner," Emmett said, looking and sounding a little apologetic.

Miller went to his desk, sat down and swung the chair around. Now his expression was a little less genial. "Matt; you're being foolish in more ways than one. In the first place if there's been murder done, you can bet your bottom dollar it won't end just because you beat a confession out of someone. There'll be others willing to take up the murdered man's cause. That leads to more killing an' the thing snowballs. In the second place, that man you just knocked senseless happens to be the right hand man of Doc Farraday, who packs more weight in these parts than anyone else does now, or ever has. What you boys have done tonight is place yourselves

61

between two grindstones."

Matt dropped his face and brought up his soggily bandaged left hand. He sat impassively working the knuckles. Emmett knew the look and the mood. Miller could keep them there until hell froze over and Matt wouldn't say a word or change his stand.

"Sorry, Sheriff," Emmett murmured. "But one thing you're wrong about; isn't anyone going to waylay Thompson over this killing."

Miller chewed on that for a while. He was far from a fool and he had his ways of ferreting things out. With men like this pair of rugged strangers who hadn't scattered their tracks around much in the past twenty-four hours, it wouldn't be too difficult to find out where they'd been and to whom they'd talked. Wouldn't be difficult at all.

"So am I sorry," he said to Emmett, got up out of his chair and plucked a big brass key off a nail driven into the wall. "Sorry because if I don't lock you boys up there's sure enough to be a killing. You made Mike Thompson look pretty bad out there in the roadway tonight. In fact, between the two of you, the whole Farraday gang looked pretty bad."

Matt's head shot up. He stared at Sheriff Miller. There was an angry red welt up the right side of his face where a fist had gouged.

"Lock *us* up," exclaimed Matt, coming up to his feet. "You let a murderer ride out of your town tonight, Sheriff, but you want to lock *us* up. Just what kind of lawman are you, anyway?"

Miller, holding that brass key in his left hand, gazed steadily at Matt. "Maybe not the best," he said quietly. "But at least you'll be alive to eat supper tomorrow night. If I left you boys loose I don't think you'd make it to dinner, let alone supper. As for Thompson; don't fret about that."

Matt's black stare sharpened towards the lawman. "Why not?" He demanded. "The second he's able he'll hear what was said out there, get astride a fresh horse and hit the trail."

"I don't think so," retorted Sheriff Miller in his unperturbed manner. "But even if he did, he wouldn't get very far."

"You mean you'd let him run?" Emmett asked, also arising.

Sheriff Miller inclined his head. "Sure would, Mister Ray, sure would. Let me explain some of the simple facts of life to you boys. Maybe your folks told you all about the birds an' the bees, but I doubt if they told you that when a feller's accused of murder in this world, his accuser's got to prove him guilty beyond any reasonable doubt. You understand?"

Emmett said, "Go on; what's the rest of it?"

"Well now; you boys don't want to cooperate with the law, so the law'll have to hold you—to be sure you're around when there's a trial—and it's also got to accept the burden of provin' you weren't just shootin' off your mouths about Mike Thompson bein' a murderer. Now then; the best way to convince me an' Doc Farraday, and a jury of twelve men, Mike *did* break the law, is for him to give himself away by running. Nothing ever looks as bad for a criminal as tryin' to escape the law. *Now* do you understand?"

Emmett looked at Matt. "Be damned," he murmured. The way Sheriff Miller had explained it, made good sound common sense. Matt exchanged looks with both of them, flexed his swelling and stiffening left hand a little and finally asked a question.

"Did you figure out Thompson was the one Em meant when he asked about a murderer earlier today, Sheriff?"

Miller wagged his head. "No. I just sort of kept an eye on you two. After we met at the saloon I figured something was brewing. Emmett was as uncomfortable as a toad on a hot stove until I walked away. I cut around back, come up on the north side and kept back there out of sight in the darkness. Even after I heard you challenge Mike, I waited." Miller made a little deprecatory gesture. "I like a good fight now and then. I should've stopped it maybe, but, well—Mike Thompson's no great favorite of mine anyway. Plus I wanted to hear someone say just who this here murderer was. So now I know. So now I've got my work cut out for me. All I'm lacking boys, is the victim's name. You ready to supply me with it yet?"

"Go ahead," Emmett said. "Tell him the whole story, Matt. What the devil—he's goin' to find out anyway. Besides, why shouldn't we just let the law handle it?"

"Because I've seen his kind of law handle things like this before, Em. Thompson'll get off. You heard him say Farraday's got more power around here than anyone else."

"And you figure to settle with Thompson for the victim?" Asked Sheriff Miller. "Matt; all you're going to do is stir up bad trouble, maybe get yourself killed, and in the end the law'll still move in."

Matt continued to work his injured hand. He appeared to be grudgingly coming around when the door was abruptly thrown open and Doc Farraday himself stepped into the room, his hawkish, lean features showing dark in the quiet light of the place. He stared straight at Matt ignoring Emmett and the lawman. With one hand he eased the door closed and took his stance in front of it.

"Grady," he said icily, "it won't work. What you're trying to do is make trouble for me. Well, let me warn you—it not only won't work, but if you're still in the Lodgepole country this time tomorrow night, I'll make it a personal point to see that you learn your lesson the hard way."

"Hold on a minute," said Dave Miller.

"Keep out of this, Dave," said the cold-eyed cattleman. "This pair of saddle tramps just tried to frame Mike Thompson by beating him senseless, then brow-beating one of my other men into saying Mike shot a damned Indian kid yesterday. It's a lie, Dave."

Emmett said, "Is it, Mister Farraday; are you sure it's a lie?"

"You know it's a lie," snapped the cowman. "I know what you two are angry about—because I ruffled your feathers a little yesterday when I caught you trespassing. But this—this framing a man for murder—this is going too far. If you want to fight my men, I'll stand for that—and maybe afterwards I'll even pay for your lousy coffins—but if you think for one minute you can—"

"Farraday," Matt interrupted to ask. "Just where were you yesterday when that kid was shot? After Em and I left you and your men, unless you rode away and left the others, you know doggoned well Thompson saw a couple of kids stalkin' a wounded doe and shot at them."

"I don't know any such thing!" Roared Farraday.

"Then how come you to just now say it was an *Indian kid* that got shot, Farraday? No one else in this room knew what kind of person got shot yesterday." Matt stopped flexing his bruised hand. He stood trading black stares with Doc Farraday; for a while the office was so still sounds drifted in from the saloon across the road. Then it was Sheriff Miller who spoke up, his voice as

65

quiet and calm as ever.

"Doc; I'm satisfied about one thing. There's been a shooting. I aim to find out what happened. You can help by answering the question Grady just asked you."

Farraday's weathered, sun-bronzed face got granite hard. He continued to glare at Matt and Emmett a moment longer before he turned a little and faced Miller. "Last night one of the men told me that after I rode off to look at a waterhole, Mike and the others rode northward to have a look at some calvy heifers and came upon a couple of hunters. Mike said they wouldn't bother running them down, got off his horse and fired over their heads to scare them."

"Yeah," growled Matt bitterly. "How far over their heads, Farraday? I spent the night with that kid. He was shot below the ribs through his soft parts. He died about two-thirty this morning. That's murder."

"I don't believe you!" Exclaimed the cowman, glaring.

"You don't have to believe me, Farraday. Or you either, Sheriff. All you've got to do is to bring Mike Thompson and those other men in here and question them. Then all you've got to do is go up where that little kid'll be buried by now, and look at the bloody rags and the tear-swollen faces of his people."

"That's fair enough," said Sheriff Miller mildly, looking straight at the cowman. "Doc; you don't hold with murder any more than I do. If Mike did that—"

"If he did," snarled Farraday, "then it was a pure accident."

"And lousy marksmanship," put in Emmett, not believing for a moment a man of Mike Thompson's caliber was that poor a shot. "But one thing remains, Mister Farraday—the kid is dead."

"Damned trespassers," Farraday growled at Emmett. "Sioux cow thieves. I know 'em. They don't hit anyone else around here—just me. I know their kind."

"A little boy is still a little boy," stated Emmett, remembering the way those anguished black eyes had tried so bravely to smile at him. "Since when do men like you an' that lousy rangeboss of yours have to make war on little kids?"

"You," ground out Doc Farraday, "just said enough, mister. I'll see you eat those words one at a time!"

"Slack off, Doc," warned Sheriff Miller. "Don't make threats. Now I'll lay it squarely on your lap: Either you bring Thompson in first thing in the morning, or I'll get up a posse and come out after him. It's your choice."

"Posse," stormed Farraday contemptuously. "Your town posses, Dave, couldn't drag a sick man out of bed. You show up at my place with a bunch of your—"

"Doc; if you want I'll fetch in the army," Miller stated, his voice for the first time showing an edge. "I'm tryin' to be reasonable, but if you don't want to play that way I'll be just as bull-headed as you are. Now put up or shut up—give me your word you'll fetch Mike in here tomorrow morning, or not. Just yes or no."

Farraday faced Sheriff Miller through a rugged long silence. He put a hand behind him as though to wrench open the door. Miller stepped forward, his face unchanged but his eyes suddenly alight with a surprising look of ferocity.

"I want your answer, Doc, and I want it right now. Do you bring Mike in or do I get up a posse and come after him?"

"I'll bring him in," snapped Farraday, spun, tore open the door and went out into the pale-lighted night.

Miller reached, caught the door and eased it closed.

When he faced back around he was as relaxed-looking as ever. "Maybe," he said quietly to Matt, "I can understand why you didn't want to talk about it, but regardless of that, I'm banking that if *you're* right—that Thompson didn't shoot high—then I'm also right, and Mike's on the run right now, which'll be all the proof *I* need, whether it'll be enough for Doc Farraday or not."

Emmett's brows drew into a perplexed frown. "You still think you can overtake him if he's got a six hour start, Sheriff?"

"I think so, Mister Ray. But just to make sure I'm going to offer you two a proposition: I'll deputize the pair of you, then you ride out tonight, while it's too dark for Farraday or any of his men to see you, and watch the ranch. If Thompson hasn't already headed out—you let him go. Let him make a real flight of it. When he's at least ten miles away, you arrest him in my name and bring him in."

"I thought you were going to lock us up," stated Matt.

Sheriff Miller crossed to his desk, dug out two battered steel stars and turned back around before he answered that. "I was—until Farraday walked in here breathin' fire. Now I think you'll be a heap safer with lots of countryside to maneuver in. Here; pin 'em on if you like, or pack 'em in your pockets. And one more thing; keep in touch with me."

"How?" Asked Emmett. "If we're trackin' Thompson into strange country, just how are we supposed to be able to—?"

"Matt'll figure that one out," said Miller, smiling a little at Grady. "Be careful. Be *damned* careful. Maybe you think, because you beat Thompson tonight on your terms, he's not a bad one. Well; if you got that notion, get rid of it. He's plenty bad. Now go get saddled up, and good luck."

Sheriff Miller opened the door and held it open until Matt and Emmett had passed through, out into the late night.

9

THEY GOT THEIR HORSES AND LEFT LODGEPOLE WITH the moon far down its distant track, riding northwesterly as though heading back up into the forest where they'd been the night before. But this was because they'd discussed the possibility of being watched in town, and afterwards also being followed. They were satisfied Doc Farraday was angry enough to do something rash, and they knew for a fact he had men among his cowboys who wouldn't hesitate to take a long shot if the opportunity presented itself.

But no one was following them. They ascertained that easily enough by halting, dismounting and pressing close to the ground for vibrations. There were none.

By the time they got close enough to make out the nearest trees Emmett said he thought it must be close to four o'clock. Matt scoffed. "Can't be more'n two-thirty," he said. Emmett didn't argue but he'd have bet money it was much later.

Matt rode up into the trees, stepped down and waited for Emmett to do the same. Then they both made a smoke, lit up behind hatbrims and squatted there doing their thinking out loud.

"He'll be gone by now," muttered Matt, peering southward. "One of us should've asked Miller if Farraday keeps skulking out on to that big plain and a dog picks up our scent and gets the ranch awake. No place to hide out there."

"Too dark for 'em to catch us," stated Emmett. "Besides, if he's—"

Matt struck Emmett's forearm with an out flung hand at the same time hissing for silence. Emmett pushed out his cigarette, rose up very carefully as Matt also came upright off the ground, and strained to catch some sound. He didn't pick it up until Matt turned from the waist and pushed his arm out.

It was a rider moving slowly through the yonder forest. He seemed to be moving down country from the direction of the Sioux camp. He rode as a man might who was not familiar with the country he was passing through, and this brought looks of frowning inquiry to the faces of both listeners. If this rider was one of the Indians he'd know the country. Obviously, it wasn't one of the hunters, which posed an intriguing question: Who was it?

They stepped to their horse's heads and rested tensed fingers across each beast's nostrils ready to clamp down hard at the first fluttery movement indicating the horses might nicker when they caught the strange animal's scent.

But the rider wasn't coming down to the tree fringe in their direction after all. He paused for a long time, then swerved and went riding off westerly. Matt relinquished his hold, stepped ahead and peered through the surrounding gloom. For as long as they could distinctly hear those movements they were still and silent, but when they finally faded out Matt turned with a quizzical expression.

Emmett answered with an equally as puzzled look. "It wasn't one of the hunters," he said softly. "That's danged sure. And it wouldn't have been Thompson—

he'd have been ridin' fast and *away* from here, not down in this direction." Emmett stepped over to his horse's side. "Let's do a little nosing around."

They rode off westerly making their way slowly, halting often to listen for the other horseman, then going on again. When they finally lost the other rider entirely, Matt suggested they hide their horses and go on afoot, which they did, but after an hour they stopped altogether; there was no further sign of the stranger at all.

"Can't quite figure it," Matt muttered. "The way he was riding I'd say he didn't know this country any better'n we do. If that's so—then what's he doin' prowling around here in the night?"

Emmett had no answers either. They returned to their horses, rode back to where they'd lost the mysterious stranger, and on out southward to the very fringe of the forest. Matt jutted his chin.

"We're about due north of Farraday's place." He was briefly silent, then he said, "Something else puzzles me, Em. If Farraday's as four-square as Dave Miller believes, then why's he tryin' to shield Thompson?"

"I didn't get the impression that he was tryin' to shield Thompson as much as I got the feeling he just resented you and me—and Miller—pushin' that murder charge at him like we did. Those big, rich cowmen are like that sometimes, Matt. And you've got to admit we pushed him."

"Too bad about him," mumbled Matt dourly. "How about the kid?"

Emmett, during this halt, had made a close study of the star lighted onward prairie. Now he said, "We can get closer than this. As I recall, the buildings were a long mile or better onward."

They rode ahead once more, but now, instead of simply watching their onward trail, they turned occasionally to also peer backwards. Somewhere behind them was that unknown other rider.

"I'll tell you one thing about that stranger," Matt said tartly. "He wasn't ridin' blind in the pit of the night just because he likes to. That feller's up to something, and I'll give you a hundred to one in spades, he's not too worried about stayin' inside the law, either."

Emmett didn't argue nor comment. He was intently watching the land which ran endlessly onwards, south and west and east of where they were. In broad daylight they could be spotted easily by any other rider. Also, they were now nearly a mile off the forest; they could be cut off if they tried reaching the trees again, if anyone was out here with that in mind.

"Hold it," whispered Matt, swinging his head left to right. "I think our stranger's coming." But almost before he'd completed this statement, Matt began to shake his head and motion for Emmett to ride off easterly. "No. No; it's comin' on from the direction of the ranch. One rider. You hear him?"

Emmett heard him. They walked swiftly off to their left being careful to minimize their noise, but the oncoming man was hurrying; he wouldn't hear them in all probability anyway.

"Thompson," Matt said softly, and reached for the upthrust butt of his saddle gun.

"Leave it be," stated Emmett swiftly. "You heard what Miller said. Give him lots of room to make his break in."

Matt didn't take his hand off the Winchester though, as they sat there gradually swinging their heads at the sounds of a horseman hurrying through the westerly

72

night.

Emmett, placing how that invisible man was bearing away from them, leaned over suddenly and said, "Matt; five'll get you ten if that's Mike Thompson, he's riding to meet that other feller."

Matt withdrew his hand from the carbine and looked around with a puzzled expression. He could understand the logic of what his pardner had just suggested. What he couldn't fathom yet was why Thompson would be riding to meet that other horseman.

"Friend?" He asked. "One of the Farraday riders gettin' in late? Em, this doesn't make too much sense; Thompson knows by now we know he shot the kid. He probably even knows Farraday and Miller also know it. Now's no time for him to be gallivantin' around like he didn't have a worry in the world."

Emmett said nothing. For a while the pair of them just sat there. They could no longer hear that rider bearing westerly and away from them. After a careful look around Emmett said, "Let's do a little sleuthin', Matt. As deputy sheriffs of a place we didn't even know existed two days ago, we got the right."

They went westerly trying to pick up the sounds of the rider they'd seen last, failed to do this and at Matt's suggestion went back up into the first belt of trees where chances of them being spotted were practically nonexistent. Here too, with spongy pine needles layered underfoot, they scarcely made a sound. Still, westward another mile, Emmett got uneasy and whispered they should hide the horses and scout on foot. Matt agreed, they found an ideal little secluded place, left their animals, took only their carbines, and went on again.

Several things were obvious now; the most critical was that since the rider from the Farraday place as well as that unknown rider had both been heading west at the same hour, they were going to meet. And secondly, if the Farraday man was really Mike Thompson, then Emmett and Matt were stumbling into something foreign to them. Finally, if that Farraday rider wasn't Thompson—they were in trouble, for clearly the time they were spending on this bizarre affair of the mysterious riders in the night, could also be the same valuable time a murderer might be escaping in another direction.

Emmett, when they paused once to listen, whispered of these things. All he got back from Matt by way of acknowledgement was a nod, a grunt, and a raised right arm pointing more northerly than westerly.

"Up there somewhere," Matt said.

"You hear 'em?"

"Nope. Smell 'em. They're smokin'. Come on."

Matt was right, but not until they'd traveled another hundred or so yards up through the forest did Emmett catch the pleasant aroma of tobacco smoke. Farther still, and they saw the men. Both were about the same build and size, at least they appeared that way in the gloom, and both were smoking as they conversed. They were standing just ahead of a particularly dense growth of bull pine. There was very little light here.

Emmett faded out behind a tree with Matt off on his left some eight or ten feet behind another tree. The blurry strangers were just far enough away so that their low conversation was tantalizingly indistinct.

For a minute Emmett and Matt looked, and strained to hear, failed dismally at both, then Matt jerked his head and the pair of them faded out Southward. Where they came together again Matt put his mouth to Emmett's ear.

"Their horses are around here somewhere. They'll tell us something. Em; there's no way of gettin' up close enough to hear what they're sayin' without walkin' right out on to them. Let's find the horses."

This proved easier than either of them expected. Both animals were tied down where prairie and forest met; down where the man from the forest had obviously waited at this pre-arranged place, for the rider from Doc Farraday's place.

Matt strode boldly up, leaned a little and pointed at the left shoulder of a big bay gelding. "Farraday's mark," he said. "I recollect it from when we first met that old cuss and his crew."

Emmett moved around the rawboned, big jug-headed sorrel the other rider had used. There were two brands, one on the right hip, big and crudely burned in as though the hand guiding that iron had been more experienced at branding cattle than horses, and a much neater, smaller brand also on the left shoulder. Neither mark was familiar to Emmett. "I'd guess either Montana or Idaho marks," he said, but shrugged his shoulders. "But I sure wouldn't bet any money on it. Anyway; I've never seen either brand before." As Emmett spoke he moved closer to examine the saddle. "Hey," he murmured. "Bedroll and saddle pockets on this one." Matt came over, stepped to the off side and began rummaging in a saddlebag. Moments later he drew forth something pale and held it up.

"Em," he hissed, "come 'round here."

What Matt was holding was a canvas pouch with the faded lettering upon it of an eastern Montana bank. The pouch was small, reinforced at the corners with leather, and had a lace-through flap which was not now closed.

"Empty," said Matt, shaking the pouch upside down.

"What d'you make of that?"

Emmett fingered the pouch, considered the obvious implications of such a thing in a night rider's saddlebags, and said, "Buckle the bag back the way you found an' let's get out of here."

Later, safely away from those two horses, his thoughts crystallizing, Emmett led Matt down to a break in the trees near the soft-lighted prairie, and halted. "Just pure guesswork," he said, "but I'd say the feller who had that pouch—and who makes a point of ridin' around in the night secretly meetin' other nightriders— is no preacher of the Holy Gospel, Matt. Stuff the pouch in your pocket. Next time we see Dave Miller give it to him. He can run it down. Now let's get back and see if we can't at least identify that feller ridin' the Farraday horse."

They started back, had gone about a hundred feet, when Matt signaled for a quick halt. Emmett came on beside him. "Leaving," Matt whispered. "Listen."

Emmett heard it; the two riders were back astride and were heading deep into the forest. Evidently the Farraday rider was not going back to the ranch.

10

MATT WAS FOR TRAILING THE HORSEMEN ON FOOT BUT Emmett opposed it. "For all we know they're bound out of the country. Hell; they could be goin' on right over those highest passes. Where'd that leave us if we were on foot?"

Matt went back after their animals with Emmett but he wasn't pleased about it. "Lose 'em for sure now," he growled. But just before they got back to the place where their animals were secreted, his face cleared. "Em; they were heading straight north."

"I know that. Never mind talking, just get untied and let's get back on the trail."

"Wait a minute, Em. You realize how far west we are?"

"Of course. Matt, for gosh sake—"

"Listen a minute will you?" Matt insisted. "If they keep going straight north, Em, they're going to ride smack dab into that big meadow where the hunter camp is. Now hell—they wouldn't do that. If one of them is Mike Thompson he surely wouldn't risk ridin' in among those Sioux—not after tippin' over Black Cloud's little boy."

"Then they'll cut off somewhere," said Emmett irritably as he swung up and started reining away. "An' if you want to stand there all night puzzlin' this thing through, do it by yourself." Emmett went riding westward again, back over the same route he'd just traveled afoot.

Matt got astride and reined off westward, but as he rode along, Matt's brow was deeply furrowed. Something here didn't make good sense to him. Either that *wasn't* Thompson up there with the stranger, it was some other Farraday rider who didn't know there'd been a killing, or else, as Emmett had said, those two would fork off the main trail somewhere.

Emmett's worries, though, were becoming less concerned with the two onward horsemen, and were becoming more concerned with a fresh peril. The sky was softly brightening along towards new day.

The forest was as good a hiding place as he and Matt could hope for in daylight, but it wasn't good enough. Not with wary horsemen traversing it, and once those two up there got wind of the fact that they were being trailed, it would be the simplest thing in the world for them to step behind a pair of trees and with their weapons, empty a pair of saddles.

Emmett was in the lead when they came to the recognizable spot where they'd last seen those two men talking and smoking. He halted to listen, then turned northward. Matt came up to say in a gruff growl: "Take it slow an' easy. This stalkin' business can change around awful easy."

For a half hour as they went along the world remained wispily dark, then even in the forest it began to softly brighten. With that brightness the peril of course increased.

Where little clearings appeared, they carefully skirted around them staying back in the trees, where the trail became wide and well-marked, Matt dismounted to rummage for the fresh tracks he invariably found.

"Straight for that damned meadow," he said. "Em; this doesn't smell right. They got to know those hunters are camped up there. Anyone ridin' through here'd see that camp."

Emmett, just as puzzled, said nothing. He only led the way. Matt followed, and after a while became so certain of their destination he no longer got down to quarter for sign.

They emerged upon the identical stony point where Blackie had brought them twenty-four hours or more, earlier, and while night gloom lingered up where they were, down in the meadow there was a bluish, soft dawn light that sparkled off dewy grass and dark green pine limbs.

" 'Be damned," muttered Emmett. "Look there, Matt. Not a teepee. No sign of the Sioux or their horses. Just cattle."

Matt dismounted and stood at his horse's head looking down. What Emmett had said was glaringly true. Except for an occasional brush shelter, the meadow looked abandoned. Perhaps a hundred fat heifers and steers were grazing upon the same grass the hunting party's horses had used only a day or two before.

"Em," Matt said softly, "I'd forgotten. They wouldn't have stayed here. Not after someone died in this place. They'd move their camp. It's the custom. Not just with the Sioux but with most redskins. After rocking up the body they'd leave this place and never come back to it. I never thought of that."

Emmett also got down. He digested Matt's observation but this wasn't what was now intriguing him. After a while he yawned, scratched his belly and gave his head a sardonic shake.

"If I've got this figured right, Matt, then Mike Thompson's lower'n I thought he was."

"What're you talking about?"

"See those cattle? There weren't any cattle in the meadow the other night. I didn't even smell any on the ride up here. They didn't all just up an' decide to walk in here yesterday either, not that many. There's about a hundred head of choice critters down there. They were cut out and driven up in here an' I'll lay you a sizeable bet they got Farraday's mark on 'em. Now then, Matt, that nightrider we came on to was riding to that rendezvous with that Farraday rider to tell him something—maybe that the cut had been made, maybe that it was time to push on with these stolen critters, to wherever they peddle 'em."

"All right, but what's that got to do with Thompson bein' lower'n you thought he was?" Asked Matt, folding his legs under him and leaning from the waist as he gazed down into the soft-lighted and brightening meadow.

"Thompson's a Montana man, Matt. Montana men know Sioux custom; they'd have to. They've grown up with these Indians. Let's say this was the best—maybe the *only*—worthwhile holdin' ground for rustled beef anywhere within a couple day's drive of the Farraday ranch. And suddenly a band of nomad hunters took it over. Thompson and his pardners would have to figure some way to get the Indians out of here or give up their rustlin' business. They'd know about that Sioux custom of never stayin' where someone had died. Matt; Thompson didn't try to shoot over that kid's head—he saw an opportunity to get the Indians out of his holdin' ground and he took it. *He deliberately killed that boy!*"

Matt continued to study the lower down land, for all the indication that he'd heard Emmett he gave, Emmett might have been mentioning the weather or the price of beef, or even the fact that he was hungry, which he undoubtedly was. Finally Matt pointed over against the northward curve of forest where a pencil-thin little wisp of grey smoke was beginning to rise up.

"Breakfast fire," he said. "The question is—do we go after them now, or do we go back and get Miller?"

"Go back," said Emmett immediately. "We've already seen two of them and there's got to be at least two more—maybe twice that many for all we know. The pair of us wouldn't stand much of a chance if they got wind of us skulkin' around on their trail."

Matt dropped his arm but made no move to arise. He kept soberly watching the forest fringe over where the fire was sending up its little grey spiral of smoke. "If we knew where Blackie and his friends went and how far off they are now, maybe we wouldn't have to go all the way back to Lodgepole. Seems like a waste of time to me, Em."

"Don't worry, Matt. Even if they start movin' those critters out right after breakfast, fat cattle travel almighty slow in country as rocky and steep as this. We'll catch up to them again."

"To hell with the cattle," mumbled Matt, still gazing downward. "I want Mike Thompson." He stood up, struck dirt and pine needles from his trousers, turned and gazed a moment at his pardner. "I reckon you're right," he said quietly. "I never thought Mike was that poor a shot. But I think your reason for him killin' the kid is right. And like you said—that makes him lower'n any man's got a right to sink, and still live. Let's go."

They got back across leather, turned and started back towards the lowlands. The morning was chilly now. The sun was up somewhere, but it hadn't more than lent a little brightness to this uplands country. Emmett buttoned his jumper and Matt turned up his collar.

Over their right shoulders stood that high up snowfield. The sun was striking up there, turning the glistening whiteness to a pale, pale pink. Elsewhere, gloomy pine trunks, dark and rough and standing in random ranks, contributed to the cold mistiness of the forest.

The trail they followed out of the forest was the same one they'd used to get into it. Once, Matt twisted backwards in his lead position to say, "Em; there must be other ways to reach that meadow. I can understand that all right, but what's puzzlin' me is just how Thompson manages to get those fat cattle cut out and driven up in there without Farraday seeing anything."

"Thompson's old Farraday's rangeboss, isn't he?" Emmett said. "Who'd know better how to scatter Farraday's riders and get the owner to go to town for supplies or something? Matt; whatever we think of Thompson, give the devil his due—he's been operating his rustlin' enterprise some little time, from what I've heard Miller an' others say, which means he's got it worked down to a foolproof business."

"Except for the kid and the hunting party," mumbled Matt, and squared back around in the saddle as they came back to familiar country again.

Out through the trees Farraday's grasslands empire lay sun lighted and serene. There was no movement anywhere out there, which was deceptively inviting to the pair of riders. If they dared cut diagonally across Farraday's land they could reach Lodgepole a lot quicker than if they had to skulk northward up and around where the mountains cut abruptly away from their down country destination.

"I say risk it," Matt stated, where they came together in the final belt of trees and sat their horses gazing outward. "No one in sight anyway."

Emmett nodded and urged his horse out into the pitiless glare of warming sunlight. They rode at an alternating lope and fast walk for several minutes. The heat was a blessing, meager though it still was at this early hour, after the pre-dawn chill of the forest. Their animals loosened with each step, warming to their work and, sensing their homeward destination, putting more heart into it than they'd done previously. In this manner they got a goodly distance from the forest and were swinging easterly before Emmett barked a small curse and pointed with a rigid arm.

"The same damned thing all over again," he said.

Dead ahead, fanning out as they'd done several days previously, were riders. Six this time, and more businesslike in their manner of spreading the line to

82

intercept Emmett and Matt.

"How does that old devil do that?" Matt growled. "Just seems to come poppin' up out of the ground."

Emmett made a shrewd guess. "Tell you what I think, Matt. I think Farraday's discovered rustlers have hit him again an' he's dustin' it over the range huntin' for 'em. The trouble is, he's dustin' in all the wrong directions and meanwhile his rustlers are squattin' around their grub fire sippin' coffee and havin' a quiet smoke."

"Well," Matt said, drawing rein. "Maybe *they're* all comfortable and peaceable, Em, but from the way those boys out there are gettin' set to receive us, I say we're in pretty bad shape."

Farraday's men were drawing their saddle guns. They had a line established across the plain nearly two hundred yards long. As before, they were keeping an eye cocked upon the stocky horsemen in the center of their line who hadn't bothered to draw any weapons.

"The king-bee himself," Matt growled, staring hard at that central figure on ahead. "And I'll make you a bet he's already recognized us."

Emmett, philosophical under some circumstances, had difficulty being that way now. "He's thinkin', since we're out here the same time he's lost more cattle, we're his rustlers, or at least part of 'em."

"What he's thinkin'," stated Matt crisply, "is that there isn't a tree closer than the forest to hang us to, Em. Maybe we can talk our way out of this. Maybe we can't, too. I sized Farraday up last night in Miller's office. If you got anythin' to say to him you better talk fast an' loud because he's a man who moves first and looks second."

"We can show him his cattle and his rustlers too."

Matt, slowing his horse still more as he and Emmett

83

came within hailing distance of those rigidly waiting
armed men blocking their passageway to Lodgepole,
made a deep down grunt which could have meant
anything—or nothing.

Farraday turned his head and gave a sharp order to
the men flanking him. At once five carbines lifted, were
snugged back against five strong shoulders, and
remained aimed.

"Hold it," Emmett cried out, uncertain of Farraday's
intentions, unwilling to believe he'd shoot two men in
cold blood but not quite convinced he wouldn't. "Hold
it, Mister Farraday."

The cowman's crisp answer came back. "Throw
down your guns. All of them."

"Wait a minute," Emmett called. "We got something
to tell you."

Farraday turned, spoke to the man on his right, and a
second later a Winchester's sharp, hard snarl shattered
the golden morning. Emmett's horse didn't even
shudder; one minute he was quietly in mid-stride
unaware of any danger, the next moment he was
dropping like a stone, straight down. Emmett had plenty
of warning. He landed upright and jumped lightly clear.
From the edge of his eye he saw Matt reaching for his
booted Winchester.

"Don't," he cried sharply. "Matt—holdup!"

Farraday hadn't moved. He too was watching Matt.
He said, in a normal tone of voice which carried easily,
"Go ahead, cowboy, try it. That's what we want.
Lynching you is too good. We want you to make a gun
fight out of this. I like my rustlers cut to pieces by
gunfire, not throttled by lariats. Get clear of him, Ray:
All right, Grady—yank it out!"

Emmett lunged across, caught Matt's arm and held

84

on. "You damned fool," he gasped. "Draw that thing an' you'll be doin' exactly what he wants!"

11

MATT'S FACE WAS BLACK WITH ANGER. IN FRONT OF him several hundred feet sat grim Doc Farraday, patiently waiting. Emmett, feeling the tightness leaving his pardner's arm, slackened his hold, turned to gaze over where those six armed men were stonily watching.

"Farraday you damned fool," he called. "We're not your rustlers, but we can—"

"Rustlers?" Snapped the cowman. "If you're not part of them how did you know I'd been hit by rustlers, Ray?"

Emmett was poised to reply when the cowman swung his head and gave an order. At once two of his cowboys lowered their carbines, booted them, lifted their reins and urged their mounts out straight ahead. As these men approached Farraday called out.

"I said throw down your weapons and I meant it. Get rid of them!"

Emmett, watching the riders coming, put his right hand upon the stock of his six-gun. Matt, however, stopped him from drawing the gun to discard it.

"Don't Em," Matt growled. "Don't touch it. That's all the excuse these two need to start shooting. Keep your hand clear." As he said this, Matt also raised his own hands; he folded both arms across his chest and put a cold, malignant look upon the pair of approaching men. They were coming up on Matt's right, which was the same side upon which Emmett was rigidly standing. When they were cutting across in front of Matt to

85

impede his sighting of Doc Farraday, one of those cowboys drew back his lips in a mirthless wide smile and said, "Do like the man says, fellers. Toss away them guns."

"You go to hell," snarled Matt. "If you want my guns, come take them."

"Smart," muttered the cowboy, still smiling. "Real smart. Well; all right, mister, you made your choice. Now me, I'd a heap rather go out with gunfire, but if you want to just twist at the end of a rope, why I reckon that's your affair."

Not until they were coming to a slow halt twenty feet away did each of those men lift his right hand from his lap. Each man had his six-gun already palmed and cocked. If Matt and Emmett had touched their guns, they wouldn't have had a chance. Matt's shrewd guess about Farraday's order to those two was proven correct.

"Get down," one of the armed men ordered, flagging at Matt with his cocked pistol. "An' do it any way you like—make a play an' die like a hero, or step down easy an' hang later. It's all the same to me."

Emmett stepped clear. Matt, without unfolding his arms, swung his right leg over the saddle horn and hit the ground on the left side of his horse. One of the range riders also dismounted. As this man started forward he said to his companion, "Watch close now, Lick. I'll disarm 'em but you keep a close watch."

The man called Lick raised his .45 and aimed it point blank. At that distance he could scarcely miss. Emmett, seeing the dismounted one heading around towards Matt, stood easy. He wasn't even looking when Matt made his play. Didn't, in fact, know anything had changed things until he saw Lick's gun hand whip sideways, Lick's face go deadly smooth and wire-tight. Then Emmett turned his head, which is all of him he moved. Across the seat of Matt's saddle he saw Matt standing straight up behind the other man. They were so close the Farraday rider's hatbrim was under Matt's nose.

"Now, mister," Matt said so softly Emmett hardly heard all the words as his pardner addressed that armed mounted man, "you just lower the gun real easy into your lap. Don't call out; don't even stiffen in your saddle. If you do, your friend dies right here."

Somehow, as that dismounted man had stepped into yank away Matt's six-gun, Matt had caught the man and swung him bodily so that his neck was in the crook of Matt's arm and his arched body was directly in front of Matt.

"Em," Matt said, still speaking very softly. "Go get Lick's gun, saunter over there easy-like. Keep him between you an' Farraday so the others won't know just yet what's happening."

Emmett moved hesitantly. He couldn't see exactly what position Matt was in because of the horse standing drowsily between them. But when he got clear of the beast's head he swung for a quick look. Matt had his gun pushed deeply into the rigid cowboy's back above the kidneys. He had his left arm bent in close about the man's throat. The cowboy's eyes were bulging in fear, his mouth was twisted as though to cry out, but he didn't make a sound.

Emmett went up on the near side of Lick and held up his hand. Lick was staring over at Matt. "The gun," Emmett said. "Be quick about it, mister." Lick turned his head like a man in a stupor. He gazed from Emmett's face to his raised hand, slowly put his cocked pistol across that outstretched palm and turned back to staring at Matt and Matt's captive.

87

"You'll never make it," he breathed.

Matt had his answer to that. "Maybe not, Lick, but tryin' is a lot better'n just giving up so you can hang us. Em; walk around the head of his horse get the other critter turned to shield me an' my friend here, then mount up."

Emmett's hopes were beginning to firm up. He got the other horse, turned it and sprang up. He now had his back to Farraday and the other mounted men far back; had those watchers cut off from their view of Matt. "Knock him over the head," he said to Matt. "Then mount up."

Matt nodded as though he'd already decided on this. As he stepped clear the cowboy he'd released made a little bleating plea. "I'm unarmed, Grady. I can't do you no harm. You don't have to knock me out."

"No," agreed Matt, and swung his .45 in a vicious little arc from behind. As the struck man's knees buckled Matt said, "I don't have to, but I'm gettin' tired of Farraday's way of doin' business; figure until he changes his tactics we won't change ours."

The mounted cowboy winced as his pardner fell. He said, "Now you tore it, Grady. Next time you won't even get this much of a chance."

Matt stepped to his horse, sheathed his gun and looked up. "We didn't have a chance anyway, and you damned well know it, mister. Just consider yourself lucky and shut up."

Matt rose up and hauled his horse around before he'd even settled over leather. At the same moment Emmett hooked the Farraday horse he was astride. They broke away into a belly-down wild run, got a full hundred feet away before someone behind them let off a howl. They were nearly a hundred and fifty feet away before any of those men back there fired at them. But after that the gunfire exploded in a wild eruption of furious sound.

Matt was in the lead, he whirled this way and that making of himself a difficult target. Emmett did the same, and because his animal was fresher, he overhauled Matt and had to hold his horse back otherwise in its fright and excitement it would have bolted leaving Matt behind.

Farraday made a common mistake. In his wrath at being out-smarted, he spurred in hot pursuit firing as he rode. All his men did the same thing too, and the chances of any of them hitting their elusive targets decreased with each wild bound of the animals under them. The hurricane deck of a saddle horse was no place to hope for marksmanship.

But anger, indignation, even humiliation at being made fools of, drove those five horsemen over the prairie like avenging angels. Once, Matt turned and fired back, but only once; he was too busy fighting to widen the lead to spend any time resisting.

Emmett's horse proved to be a swift, tough beast. He had a rough gait but each time he came back to earth he'd covered another ten or twelve feet. Ahead, the forest swept down to meet them, its inviting tangle of gloomy shadows and stiff-topped trees offering much needed sanctuary. It was Matt's intention, Emmett saw the moment they got into the trees, to head upcountry to that large meadow where the rustled cattle were. Clearly, if Farraday saw his beef, saw the men who had stolen them, he would be willing to listen to Matt and Emmett, or, if not listen, at least abandon this furious pursuit long enough for the pursued men to get away, while Farraday chased the real thieves.

Matt whipped back and forth through the trees,

leading out. Emmett, with the fresher mount, swerved out a short distance to perhaps draw at least part of the pressure off his pardner. It was good strategy, in both cases, except for one thing: Farraday and his gun firing riders burst into the forest without any hesitation. They knew this country too. But it wasn't their anger or even the grim resolve which drove them, it was their thunderous gunfire. Emmett had no idea where he materialized from, but suddenly, up ahead of Matt, Mike Thompson lunged through the trees, gun up and swinging.

Emmett yelled, and hauled at his Winchester. He looped his reins carelessly and raised the carbine. But Matt had already seen his danger. He drew and fired. Thompson, plunging straight into Matt's path, went down in a wild sprawl with his upended horse. Matt had to haul back sharply to lift his own mount over that heap of threshing hooves and arms. He made it. Emmett, converging, cut around Thompson and his horse. As he whipped on, turning eastward now to follow Matt who had been diverted into a fresh direction by this unexpected frontal assault, he caught one glimpse of Farraday's rangeboss before his horse carried him swiftly in among the eastward trees cutting off his view. Thompson had been stunned by his tumble. Emmett wasn't sure whether Matt's bullet had struck Thompson or his horse. Both were floundering there on the ground. It had actually struck neither of them. What had occurred was more complex. The bullet had sliced into the furry bark of a big fir. The bark had stung Thompson's horse in the face, in the eyes, causing it to attempt an abrupt, panicky halt. The resulting fall was the result of the beast's own legs getting entangled.

Now, Matt rowelled his horse mercilessly and

steadily widened the distance between pursued and pursuers until, fifteen minutes later, he dared draw rein and let Emmett ease in beside him.

"Any sign?" Matt demanded sharply, peering backwards.

"None," answered Emmett. "I think, when Thompson went down, it diverted them. But we'd better keep goin'."

They rode on, but at a walk now to 'blow' their mounts. Eventually, crossing an open side hill where the stillness as well as the fierce sunlight caused them to briefly halt once more, they took longer to make certain they had lost their pursuit.

Here, while his jaded horse recuperated, Matt made a smoke and lit up. He gave Emmett a wry head-wag and a raw little smile. "Close, pardner," he said through exhaled smoke. "Too close. That consarned old devil would have strung us up without givin' us a chance to explain. I figured by leadin' him up where the cattle and the rustlers were, he might at least get off our backs for a while. Then that damned Thompson came out of nowhere."

"Not out of nowhere," stated Emmett. "That was Thompson all right, last night; the one ridin' up to meet that other feller from the direction of Farraday's ranch."

"Heard the gunfire," mumbled Matt, looking expertly at his run-out horse. "Heard the gunfire and came rushin' down to divert 'em. Well; it worked. But I bet he never figured on gettin' his teeth shook loose to accomplish it."

They rode on out of the side hill clearing following the long-spending curve of the mountainside around more northerly than easterly, and even though this promised to take them a goodly distance out of their

91

way, neither of them even mentioned leaving the hills again for the open prairie.

"You reckon Farraday just might go on up anyway?" Matt asked, and when Emmett sardonically shook his head Matt agreed. "Naw; Thompson'd see to that. He'll probably keep 'em on our trail."

They did not see any more pursuit though, not even when they eventually had to leave their sheltering hill and start the long ride on down cross-country towards Lodgepole.

The sun was well up, the land swam in golden warm springtime warmth, the sky was cloudless, in every direction there was nothing to mar the onward serenity of their continuing ride, except Matt's pointed, laconic, and quite graphic description of Doc Farraday.

"Sure I'm mad," he told Emmett, "but more'n that, I'm plumb indignant. If he's half the man Sheriff Miller claims, how come him to jump the gun like that? By grabs, Em, he'd have killed the pair of us."

"He was mad about losin' those cattle."

"Well hell, every time a feller loses a few head of cattle, if he starts out to hang the first fellers he runs across, directly now there aren't goin' to be enough cowboys left to herd cattle in these parts."

Emmett grinned, but he still kept his eyes roving over the surrounding countryside, and in the end it paid a solid dividend.

"Look yonder, Matt. Back behind us an' southward about two miles. Is that the same bunch of men?"

Matt spied the bunched up party of horsemen, gauged their direction and speed, hauled his brows down into that black scowl of his and swore. "It's them all right. Old Farraday leadin' his wolf pack towards Lodgepole. Now we dassn't try to reach town first or he'll spot us sure, and maybe next time he'll be the lucky one."

They halted far northward, got down and stood beside their horses to minimize the chances of being seen. It worked. Those loping small specks down country swept right on across their front and never changed direction nor altered their gait as they hastened along.

"Wonder if Mike's still with 'em?" Matt mused.

Emmett had his doubts. "He wouldn't dare go into town with Sheriff Miller layin' for him on that murder charge. But I'll bet you one thing: I'll bet you he talked Farraday out of making him show up at Miller's jailhouse like Farraday promised Miller."

Matt got quiet now. He was evidently trying to surmise how their abrupt presence in the neighborhood would affect not just Doc Farraday, but those upcountry cow thieves as well, because surely, if Thompson had left Farraday back in the forest, he'd hurried back to warn his rustler-friends of danger.

12

THERE WAS NOTHING FOR IT, UNLESS THEY WISHED FOR another encounter with Doc Farraday and his crew, but to let the cowman reach Lodgepole first. This they did by taking their time at riding down country. When they were well within sight of town their horses were completely rested and even they, themselves, felt no lingering after-effects of that wild chase.

There was no sign of Farraday on ahead, but where the stage road came down from the northward hills a growing cloud of dust indicated riders from that direction, at least. Emmett thought it might be a stage. Matt didn't pay much attention. Riders or a coach, it did not appear to have much bearing on them, and Matt said so.

They were within a half mile of town before that dust cloud crystallized into a band of riders. Emmett and Matt stopped to watch.

"Pretty big party of 'em," Matt said.

Emmett said nothing until he got a good look. "Posse, Matt. There are too many to be cowboys headin' for town from some outlyin' ranch."

They headed over closer to the stage road where the big body of riders was swinging southward. When it was eventually possible to ascertain individual men in that large band of horsemen, Matt pointed at a rider out front. "Miller," he said, and instantly hooked his horse sending the animal forward in a startled rush. Emmett gigged the horse he was riding too. At about that time the posse men noticed them and distant calls ran up and down the line as men slowed and pointed westerly. Sheriff Miller hauled down to a halt, gave a gruff order to the twenty and more men with him, then spurred on out to meet Emmett and Matt while his possemen remained upon the roadway.

Matt slowed and finally halted. So did Emmett. Miller loped the last few yards and when he recognized the men in front of him, made a quizzical frown.

"Where's Thompson?" were Sheriff Miller's first words, put forth even before his mount had come to a complete stop. "I thought you two were going to shag him?"

"We found him," stated Matt, and told what experiences they'd had since leaving Lodgepole the night before. "And now Farraday's down in Lodgepole waiting for you."

"With Mike?" Asked Miller.

Matt's response was dry. "I doubt it, Sheriff. The way we figure it, Mike's got to get back, warn his rustler friends and get those cattle to movin' out of the country. But even if he didn't have to do that, he still wouldn't be fool enough to let Farraday fetch him into Lodgepole so you could lock him up. But it's not Thompson we're sweatin' out right now, Sheriff, it's Farraday. We knocked one of his lads over the head. He won't overlook that. Right now he's down there in your town with five or six of his crew. There are only two of us. Before you or either one of us can go back after Thompson and those rustlers, someone's got to neutralize Doc Farraday."

Dave Miller nodded. "I'll take care of that. It just so happens that before I could wait around an' see if Doc would keep his word and bring Mike in, some men hit a passenger coach northward about six miles, robbed everyone and took the mail sacks. That's where I've been with this posse. Well; I'll keep the posse organized when we get back to town an' if twenty-five armed men can't take the snap out of Doc Farraday and five of his men, I don't know what can."

"Twenty-seven armed men," said Emmett, lifting his reins.

Miller nodded and turned his horse. The three of them rode back to the stage road where impatient horsemen were waiting. At a word from Sheriff Miller the entire big cavalcade started down country again in a looping lope that set up a dust banner a hundred feet high. As they sped along Emmett twisted for a glance at the posse men. There were cattlemen as well as townsmen in this party of armed men. They all seemed very capable. Sheriff Miller reined around until he got between Emmett and Matt then he asked loudly if either

95

of them had caught any glimpse of the cattle thieves. Neither had and Matt explained why. He also dug out that canvas pouch and handed it across, explaining how he and Emmett had come upon the thing.

Sheriff Miller was electrified at the lettering on the pouch. "I think we've bagged something much bigger than rustlers," he said loudly, waving the pouch up in front of his face. "This bank was robbed four weeks ago. It was in every newspaper in Montana Territory. There were five bandits and they shot two customers an' a clerk in their getaway. After that they dropped out of sight. Unless Mike Thompson's friend can do a lot of tall explainin' about how he came by this pouch, we're going to have us a herd of *real* outlaws in tow."

"Not until we catch 'em we aren't," stated Emmett. Then he said, "Sheriff; why not cut off towards the hills right now, with this big posse? It'd save goin' on into Lodgepole."

Dave Miller raised his right hand to point westward, high up. "See those highlands? Well; if Mike's pardners in the stolen beef business have been at it as long as I'm beginnin' to think they have, they'll have at least one man atop those high places watching just such dust clouds as we're puttin' up right now. If we left the road headin' westward, maybe we'd eventually locate the Farraday cattle, but Emmett, we'd never see hide nor hair of those renegades—includin' Thompson, if he's with them."

"If," muttered Matt, slowing his horse as they came close to the outskirts of town. "He's with 'em, Sheriff. I'll bet you a new pair of boots on that."

The posse met with a silent but searching stare from both sides of the plank walk as it came down into town. The sun was directly overhead now, the heat was noticeable but not unpleasant. It aided visibility, which offered Emmett his best chance to identify the waiting men slouching down there in front of Miller's jailhouse.

"Sheriff," Emmett said, "Farraday's waitin' in front of your office. Maybe you won't need this big posse to hunt him down with after all."

Miller looked, grunted, and shook his head. "One damned thing after another. First this Farraday-Thompson mess, then this stage robbery." The lawman suddenly scowled, lifted the canvas pouch Matt had given him, and as he examined it again he began to look speculative. "It could've been the same bunch sure as the devil," he said so softly scarcely any of the bunched up men with him heard. Matt heard all right but he didn't pay much attention, for down the road Farraday and his men had suddenly recognized Emmett and Matt in that posse and were walking out to the tie rack before Miller's jailhouse for closer looks.

When the lot of them swung in, they nearly filled the roadway on both sides of the jailhouse with their horses. As Sheriff Miller swung down, a little canvas pouch clutched in one fist, he didn't give Farraday a chance to speak first. "Doc; you distinctly told me last night you were goin' to fetch Mike Thompson first thing this morning. It's now . . ." Miller cocked an eye at the overhead sun. " . . . a little past high noon and you're not only late but I don't see any sign of Mike among your men."

Farraday and his riders were glaring savagely over where Matt and Emmett were dismounting, prudently keeping their horses turned between themselves and the Farraday outfit. "Sheriff," said the fierce cattleman, pointing rigidly. "There are your two most critical renegades right there—Grady an' Ray. They not only

97

are part of a crew that's rustlin' my beef, they also hit one of my men over the—"

"Where is Mike?" Roared Sheriff Miller, no longer his customary even-tempered self. "Doc, when a man tells me he's goin' to do somethin' I expect him to keep his word. Now where is Mike Thompson?"

Farraday seemed astonished by the lawman's sudden bellow and his angry countenance. He slowly lowered his pointing arm and turned away from Emmett and Matt. "All right," he said softly. "All right, Sheriff. I didn't bring him in."

"You had him, Doc?"

"Well. Not exactly. He wasn't at the home place this morning. I reckon he'd pulled out some time in the night. But after we caught Grady and Ray on the range, and they got away from us, we chased 'em into the trees and Mike was up there. He tried to stop Grady and Ray. One of them spooked his horse and it fell with Mike."

"Well dammit all, where is he now?" Demanded the lawman. "I know all about the rest of it. *Where is he now?*"

Farraday put a long, skeptical glance upon the sheriff. After a while he said, "Dave; you don't believe that wild tale about the Indian kid dyin' do you? Listen to me; those two over here deliberately set this whole thing—"

"Doc," said Sheriff Miller, stepping in close, grabbing Farraday's six-gun out of its holster and stepping back again, "you just put yourself in the position of a feller aidin' and abettin' a felon—Mike Thompson. You're under arrest."

Farraday was stunned. So were his men. They seemed initially disposed to fight, to free their employer with guns, but one glance around showed the folly of

98

anything like this. The posse men, also astonished, were still too numerous for Farraday's men to resist.

Sheriff Miller poked at Farraday with the cattleman's own six-shooter. "March," he said, gesturing towards his jailhouse door. Then he looked around. "You posse men—thanks. Maybe we didn't get us any stage robber, but don't think we won't get him. You can break up now an' head for home." Miller paused as he ran his eyes over the leaderless and bewildered Farraday men. "You boys—you stay out here with Grady and Ray. I'll be back as soon as I've locked up your boss. Then maybe the bunch of us'll take a little ride."

Emmett turned to Matt as Miller herded his icy-eyed and totally, grimly, silent prisoner on inside. "This Dave Miller's no fool," he muttered. "He doesn't care about that aidin' an' abettin' business. All he wants is to get rid of old Farraday so he can use his riders to hunt down Thompson and Thompson's cow-thievin' pardners."

Matt nodded. "Sort of got that notion myself," he said, and strolled over where Farraday's men were talking together in a little bunch. He picked out one man and called him by name.

"Hey Link, how's your pardner I don't see him here."

The cowboy turned and balefully stared at Matt. " 'Course you don't. He's got a headache an' the boss sent him back to the ranch. But you wouldn't know nothin' about him to get that headache, would you, Grady?"

Emmett, standing off a little, watched and listened but said nothing. One thing was obvious; without Mike Thompson or Doc Farraday, the men grouped together up there beside Miller's jailhouse door were a lot less formidable regardless of their obvious toughness and their numbers.

99

Matt hooked both thumbs in his shell belt and gazed hard at Link. "I'll tell you," he said. "I'd have told Farraday if he'd have listened—we were no part of a rustler crew. Also, Mike Thompson is a murderer. Some of you boys were with him the other day when he supposedly shot over that little kid's head. If you're stupid enough to believe Thompson was that poor shot—to hit the kid low in the side—then you're dumber than you look."

A couple of those cowboys exchanged looks but none of them spoke. Link cleared his throat, spat aside, looked over at the jailhouse door and back again. "What're you tryin' to prove?" he mumbled at Matt. "You're sayin' Mike's stealin' from the boss, as well as a murderer. All because he an' Doc Farraday jumped you'n your pardner out on our—"

"You must be the dumbest," said Matt, breaking in. "You saw Mike come out of that forest this morning when we were runnin' away from you boys. If he'd left the country last night like old Farraday said, how come he's not any farther away than he was this morning, Link? You better start usin' your skull for something besides keepin' your ears apart."

Link's heavy face got rusty with dark color. "I'm gettin' sick of your talk, feller," he said to Matt. "You got a gun on."

Emmett moved a little so as to have those other men well in sight. He didn't think a fight was coming but he was a prudent man; taking chances where armed men were concerned didn't seem like good sense to him.

Matt nodded at Link. "Yeah I got a gun on. Also I'm remembering something, Link: The way you and your pardner came on to Em an' me this morning—with cocked pistols in your laps. You know what I think of men who'd do that?"

"No," said Link, easing his body forward a little, dropping his sloping shoulders, focusing his smoldering stare upon Matt. "Tell me what you think of fellers who'd do that, Grady?"

Now Emmett saw how abruptly the atmosphere had shifted. He dropped his right hand and waited. The men behind Link, though, seemed unwilling despite the big odds, to buy into this gathering storm. They sidled out of harm's way leaving Link facing Matt.

For a moment Matt neither moved nor spoke. He had a faintly sardonic expression down around his mouth. He raised both hands and bewildered Link by this because he clearly wasn't going to draw. Then, as Link's brows furrowed and his lips parted, Matt struck. The blow didn't travel more than two feet, but its impact was like solid granite. Link's eyes flew wide open, his open lips sagged still wider, and he fumbled with his right hand out of instinct, then he fell, struck the plank walk hard and rolled once.

The Farraday riders were no less surprised than Emmett was. Matt turned, ran a sulphurous glance over the Farraday men, then said, "That about evens the score, Em. They got tough with us; we gave one a headache and now this one—well—I got an idea he's going to have a jaw-ache. But I figure he and his pardner'll think twice before they try that bushwhacker's trick of keepin' a cocked gun in the lap out of sight when you're tryin' to bait men to draw."

The jailhouse door opened, Sheriff Dave Miller stepped out, halted and gazed blankly where Link unconsciously lay.

"Never mind him," Matt said quietly. "He met with a small accident. We got a lot of ridin' to do, Sheriff.

Let's get astride and get at it."

13

THEY LEFT LODGEPOLE WITH BRIGHT SUNLIGHT ALL around them. Farraday's cowboys seemed not too averse to riding with Sheriff Miller. They didn't even act very disturbed to be riding with the men who'd not only been instrumental in getting their employer locked up, but who had also left one of their bolder companions back in town nursing a swollen jaw.

"If," one of them indifferently told Emmett, Link wasn't a real close friend to Mike, an' if Mike wasn't in trouble over a murder, maybe it'd be different. But we sort of talked this mess over last night in the bunkhouse, and the fellers felt it'd be crazy to let Farraday or Thompson drag us all into a fight where we'd be lined up square against the law."

"Good figurin'," stated Emmett, and glanced up ahead where his pardner and the sheriff were riding. Those two spoke now and then as the five of them rode along; now and then, too, Dave Miller would raise an arm to point out some landmark to Matt. He undoubtedly knew this countryside.

The direction they rode was roughly the same route Matt and Emmett had taken going out last night towards the faraway hills. From this Emmett could deduce that Matt had described that hidden uplands meadow to Miller, and the sheriff, knowing which place he'd referred to, was now leading them straight towards it.

Where they crossed Farraday range there was a vast emptiness until, within gunshot of the forest again, Matt and one of the rangeriders spotted a roil of thin dust off southward. The cowboy said, sounding a little puzzled, "That's comin' from down by the ranch buildings."

"What's odd about that?" Queried Emmett.

One of the other cowboys said, "No one's down there but the cook. Mister Farraday hires seven men. With Mike gone he's only got six. With him'n Link gone that leaves five. Us three fellers are all the Farraday riders still around. There's only the cook at the ranch like I said, an' he's too boogered-up an' old to make that big cloud o' dust. Besides, he don't ride no more, and that dust's bein' made by horses. It's movin' too fast to be cattle."

Matt put forth his hand to restrain Dave Miller as the Lawman started to lift his reins. "Wait a minute," said Matt, and sat there watching the dust, saying nothing more for a long while. "Never catch 'em anyway," he ultimately decreed. "They're heading straight for the mountains an' they're at least three miles off. All we'd do is run our horses down."

"Who you reckon that'd be?" Asked a perplexed rider. "Hell; Mister Farraday's got no friends who'd come over an'—"

"Thompson and his friends getting fresh horses," stated Matt, reining out in the same direction they'd been riding. "And that'll make things a little tougher."

They came eventually to the forest fringe, faded out up through the trees and fell into a serpentine line with Matt up front, Sheriff Miller behind Matt, and the others strung out behind Miller. There was no longer any need, or any reason, for talk. They therefore poked along in gloomy shade, being quite silent.

To Emmett, it seemed as if Thompson and his friends had indeed gone to Farraday's ranch for fresh animals, then the rustled beef couldn't be too far ahead. He also

103

thought that if Thompson had done that, he'd wasted valuable time. But in the end, he came to the conclusion that perhaps, since there was no way to push these fat cattle through the mountains at any swifter gait than a shuffling fast walk, he and his gang would be able to race back, get fresh animals, and race forward again, and still not have to strain too much.

What was critical for the rustlers was the time they'd wasted before they had any idea angry horsemen were in the hills. Now, nothing could change that delay; cattle could head up trail just so fast and no faster.

They found the trail leading to the high meadow. Matt twisted to look around the others and back down to Emmett. He wrinkled his nose. Emmett understood. There was a scent of dust in the still air meaning that horsemen had hastened up through here not too long before. Emmett nodded, Matt squared up in the saddle, and for nearly an hour the five of them kept going. Where they eventually halted, at Dave Miller's suggestion, to talk a little about their plan and what they might be riding into, was about half a mile below the big meadow.

Dave Miller put out the question among them seeking to get some fairly accurate notion of how many men they might be up against. Matt thought five. Emmett had no idea at all so Matt turned and pointed to the dusty trail. That settled it. Speeding horsemen left different fresh tracks from slow-moving riders.

"There's one thing sticks in my head," stated the sheriff. "These men are probably the same ones who robbed a bank in the western end of the territory four weeks back. If so, they're very dangerous. Also, as I've been pokin' along I've been pondering why they'd take a big risk and go out over that open range back there to

104

steal fresh horses. I think the reason they did that, is because they are also the same men who rode through the hills last night, waylaid the stage this morning, robbed it, then raced away back into the hills again. If they arc, they'd need fresh horses badly."

Emmett exchanged a stare with Matt. Neither of them had put the facts together as deftly as Miller had. But then, neither of them were concerned with that distant bank robbery or the hold-up of Lodgepole's morning coach from the north.

One of Farraday's men, in the act of making a cigarette, raised his head to look far up through the forest where a faint edge of mountaintop showed brightly golden in the afternoon light. This man said in a slow drawl, "Sheriff; you got any idea where men could drift a band o' cattle through these yere mountains?"

Miller turned to follow out the way that cowboy had looked. "There are passes," he said, "but I've got to admit that I've never been over them. I've heard of trails through the hills for a good many years, so I know all we've got to do is keep trailing them and we'll eventually—"

"I wasn't thinking like that," drawled the cowboy, his cigarette lighted now and giving off its thin little straightup bluish smoke. "I was thinkin', did any of us know the way, the thang t'do yere ain't jest poke along eatin' their dust, but cut out an' aroun' an' come down on 'em in the mouth of the same pass they're usin'. Maybe in some narrow place where they got no place to get aroun' us. Y'all understand? Cut 'em off, stop 'em cold, and rub their noses in it."

Matt was listening with an interested expression across his face. Emmett also was studying this smoking cowboy. They both recollected him as having been in that little band which had initially halted them upon Farraday's range. He was a lanky, droopy-eyed, deceptively mild appearing man—a Texan by the sound of his talk and the sleepy, slouching way he stood.

"How about you?" Matt asked the man. "You know how to get around up in here?"

The cowboy shook his head. "Sure don't, Mister Grady. But if a couple of fellers was willin' to make the effort I'd sure admire to ride with 'em."

Emmett, gently amused by the man's laconic style and drowsy attitude, raised his eyebrows at Dave Miller. The sheriff twisted to quietly study the onward landform. It was difficult to make out very much of it because the surrounding forest impeded a good sighting. But apparently Miller knew the land in a general way because as he turned back he said to Matt, "The peaks run west to northeast. I can't believe they'll push the cattle northeastward though because in that direction they're bound to run into other cowmen. Also, over there, lies the stage road, and it's fairly well traveled."

"That leaves due north, or maybe northwest," Matt muttered, twisting to look.

Miller watching Matt, said, "You game, Grady?"

Matt didn't turn back. He didn't answer. Emmett stepped up. "He's game, Sheriff. So am I. We'll take this Farraday man too. If we have any luck at gettin' around them—"

"I'll hear the shooting," said Miller wryly. "All right. Let's split up and get at it."

Matt finally turned and said, "Not yet. We'll get up to the big meadow first, then split up."

No one asked Matt why he wanted it that way. No one really cared. They got back astride and pushed straight out on to the stony ridge above the big meadow.

106

There, they halted again.

The meadow was empty, which they expected. There wasn't even any visible dust where animals had been recently pawing, but then, as Emmett observed to the others, Thompson's gang'd had at least three hours head start.

Matt moved over beside Dave Miller. From this place, with no immediate forest to impede the view, the land lay revealed in every direction except to the east, which lay on their right. It was spiked with bristly ranks of red barked old shaggy pines. The highest peak, the one with its eternal snowfield high up, was to their left. Straight ahead the forest climbed steadily, broke once, then climbed upwards again widening its sweep from east to west until, where several notches appeared along the distant rim, it ended in a top-out which lay now darkly silhouetted against a golden sky.

"Three passes up there," Matt observed, pointing to the three breaks in the skyline. "The thing we've got to guess right about first time is—which pass."

"You'll have their tracks," stated the lawman. "If I was doing this I'd stay on their trail until I knew which pass they're headin' for—then start my ride out and around them."

Matt dropped his gaze to the meadow below. Emmett, watching his pardner's face, knew Matt didn't agree with the lawman. He was right. Matt finally said, "Sheriff; they number about the same number as we do. By now they know damned well we're after them." Matt caught the reins to his horse, paused, then said as he turned to mount up. "They'll be watchin' their backtrail like eagles. All right, Em; you'n Mister Farraday's cowpuncher get astride. Let's split off an' get to riding." As he settled into his saddle Matt gazed at Miller.

"Don't push 'em too close, Sheriff. They'll ambush you sure as the devil given half a chance. See you later."

There was no other way to get down into that big meadow that either Emmett or Matt could determine, so they descended the same way they had their first time in here, with Blackie. But as Matt said part way down the exposed trail, "If Thompson just left one feller lyin' over yonder in the trees he can pick us off like crows on a fence."

But no one shot at them. Emmett hadn't believed anyone would. He didn't think Matt believed that either, for the elemental reason that Thompson would only be depriving himself of a man by having anyone remain this far behind. The Texan had no comment along these lines at all. He slouched along looking as ineffective and careless as he always seemed to look, but his small, wet stone eyes constantly flicked from place to place, searching, probing, rummaging for an enemy or the sign left behind by an enemy.

They passed through the little brush shelters, empty and sadly silent now; they also passed several stone rings where teepees had been. The brush shelters caught and held the Texan's quick interest. But those stone rings caused him to suddenly halt his horse. He pointed, saying, "Been danged redskins in here boys."

Matt kept on riding. "We know that," he said. "Come along."

The Texan obeyed, but after that he kept a close eye upon Matt as though less willing than ever to completely trust Emmett's pardner. As they moved northward across a small opening towards the continuing forest, Emmett said "Texas; don't worry about it. He hasn't lifted a scalp in couple o' weeks now. Not since he took the pledge."

The cowboy lay an unamused glance upon Emmett. "Let me tell you, mister," he said, dropping his voice. "Where I grew up we trust no redskin. Least o' all, we trust no half-blood. I been tryin' to puzzle out what your pardner reminds me of ever since we lef' Lodgepole. Well; now I know—he puts me in mind of a cussed Indian!"

Emmett gazed on over where Matt was passing into the first belt of trees. "He'll put you in mind of somethin' all right," said Emmett, "if he gets between you an' your old friend Mike Thompson. So you just keep on ridin', Texas, an' keep your thoughts about my pardner to yourself. You don't have to like either one of us. All you've got to do is fight when the time comes to fight, and meanwhile just keep riding."

That was the end of it. Whatever the cowboy privately thought, he took Emmett's sound advice and kept it strictly to himself.

Where the rustlers had taken those Farraday cattle there was a fairly good trail which wound forth and back through the trees for nearly a half mile before it swung up and over, and downward into a long trough lying east and west. Here, from the signs, they'd allowed the critters a brief rest before heading westward through that narrow slot. There was the most distant of all those upcountry notches in the westerly skyline. This answered one question to Emmett's satisfaction. He spoke of it to Matt.

"They're making for that farthest pass. There aren't any other gun sights up on that skyline, so that's the only pass through from this side."

Matt agreed. He fell to studying the onward land. "If we know that much," he said to Emmett and the Texan, "then the only other thing we've got to know is just how

109

to get up there ahead of the herd."

None of them commented. They had a fairly good view up the slot, which was grassy and more or less free of brush and trees, until it lifted and turned shadowy where the forest closed in again. From that forward spot onward up to the pass against the afternoon-speckled sky, there was only more trees, more dark places, and no visible way to get around the rustlers and up into that distant pass.

The Texan shook his head. "Hell on horses," he said. "But we got to try goin' straight up to get above 'em, then cut westward to reach the pass. Ain't no other way I can see."

He was correct. There was no other visible way.

14

MATT LEFT THEM ONCE TO SCOUT UP THE ONWARD trail on foot. When he returned he indicated that thus far at least, they were right. "Pretty good trail at that," he told them. "I'd guess it was an old hunter's route into these mountains. Old Indian trail from whatever's on the other side of these hills. It follows out through the trees along the slope so that the critters aren't actually doing much real climbing although they're constantly getting higher and higher towards that pass yonder."

"Yeah," mused the Texan. "The way the buffalo used to do. They never went straight up no slope. Too smart or too cussed for that. They'd spiral round an' round a mountain until first thing you knew, there they was on top of it—without even puffing."

"Too bad we're not buffalo," stated Emmett gazing up where they had to go.

Matt led out again. For a hundred yards they rose gradually as the grassy fold in the hills also lifted. Then, as they passed into the forest again, Matt turned off to the right. From there on it was hard climbing. It was also slow climbing; no horseman with any feeling for his animal ever forced a horse to move up more than a couple hundred feet at a time in this kind of country, without a corresponding rest. Eventually, where the slopes got too steep, too greasy with pine needles, they all three dismounted and puffed uphill beside their animals. Once, when they paused to look backward and downward, the Texan said, "Y'know; once when I was a button I had me a schoolmarm who said I'd never even get close t'heaven, and this just proves how wrong them schoolmarms can be." He craned his neck around, shook his head and said, "Be danged if I don't expect I'm closer t'heaven right now than that old biddie'll ever get."

They reached a brushy bench with sunlight burning brightly against an open place, and there they had to drop downhill in order to remain in the trees while skirting that opening. The Texan had some choice comments to make about this, but twenty minutes later when they came upon a huge old punky deadfall blocking their onward path, the Texan was so short of wind he didn't have a word to say. He simply joined Matt and Emmett, and gazed at this latest of obstacles.

They got around the deadfall but they had to sacrifice elevation again to accomplish it. Afterwards, they started right back up the slope again. They were making progress, but as Emmett observed, an old rump-sprung calvy cow with her front legs hobbled and dragging a lead weight could have cruised past them like they were tied to a tree.

111

They made a rest camp finally, where they started a big roman-nosed old cow-elk out of her bed in a thicket where lush greenery surrounded a tiny emerald spring. The horse drank, waited for the pothole to refill, and drank some more. It was hot work, climbing a mountainside with the afternoon sun beating upon it. It was also wearisome work.

Matt left Emmett and the Texan to course along the slope in the direction of that onward pass. Up here, the forest seemed more verdant; there was underbrush, more spruce and aspen among the shaggy old pines, and even some high altitude fir trees with their unshaven look. There were also chipmunks, bluejays flashing brightly overhead, and handsome, saucy gray squirrels butter-fat and irritated at this human invasion of their private domain.

Matt came back as the Texan was making a smoke. Emmett, who had just tanked up on fresh water at their little spring, was sprawling in wonderfully fragrant high-country shade. He rolled his eyes around as Matt stepped up.

"You see 'em?" He asked.

Matt made a motion at the Texan instead of answering Emmett. "Don't light that cigarette." This brought all the quick interest of both rested men up in a hurry. The Texan offered no objection at all. He simply smashed the cigarette against the ground and continued to gaze at Matt.

"I asked you," reiterated Emmett, "did you see them?"

Matt dropped to one knee. "No. Not them. But I saw something else that might interest you, Em. I saw four men on horses up there near the south end of that pass, sitting in the shade beside the trail like sentinels."

Emmett sat up. "Not Thompson?" He queried.

"Don't know. Can't say who they are," Matt stated, and swung his head as the Texan spoke.

"Where's the danged cattle? We got to know that before we can say who them fellers are."

This was palpably true. The three of them got up and faced northwestward where the pass showed against the reddening afternoon sky. "No sign of the cattle," muttered Matt. "But I didn't really go down low enough to catch sight or scent of 'em anyway."

"We got to do that," affirmed the Texan. "Listen, boys, if there's more'n just Mike's rustler friends up in here, we got to know about it. First thing we know we're goin' to ride smack-dab in between two bunches of armed fellers, an' that'll be all—"

Matt put aside his carbine and bent to unbuckle his spurs. "You two stay here. I'll go have a look." When Emmett started to argue Matt looked darkly at him. "One man makes less noise an' better time than two men. But the main thing, Em, is that nothing happens to our horses. You and Texas stay."

"And if they spot you first?" Emmett asked caustically.

Matt stood up. "You'll hear the shootin'," he said, and walked off.

It was now mid-afternoon. The sky was a series of high cloud fields resembling separate bands of grazing sheep. There was color turning the sun from hammered gold to dusty copper. That snowfield which was across an escarpment of the highest peak, was dark red and glowing like a steady, flameless fire.

There were sounds in the roundabout forest, as there always were in every forest. Movements of small, secretive animals in the darkest gloom contrasted with

113

the sharp and strident scolding of the bluejays and tree squirrels overhead. To a person familiar with this kind of country every sound was a message; a warning, an announcement, a chuckle, a grumble or a groan.

Once, Emmett thought he'd caught the sound of lowing cattle. But when he glanced around at the Texan to see whether this was so or not, his companion was sitting there, shoulders to an old tree, eyelids two-thirds closed, totally unaware of anything so portentous. Emmett decided it was his imagination and went on waiting.

A snuffling old bruin shedding his winter hair in matted clots, came down through the trees scolding and whining and bitterly complaining about his lot. Very suddenly he stopped, reared up on to his hind legs and vigorously sniffed. Because his eyes were very weak and also because neither Emmett nor the Texan were moving now, he failed to see them. They did not fail to see him though; both put forth surreptitious hands to their weapons, and waited. A gunshot now would spoil everything; would not only alert Thompson there were others in the mountains too, but would in all probability set the armed rustlers to searching, which could conceivably place Matt in great peril.

The bear had not just come out of hibernation and therefore was not as belligerent as he otherwise would have been. Still, he was lean and shedding, which meant he hadn't been out very long, so the two men sat and watched, and silently hoped for all they were worth he would not decide to start his fighting season here and now.

He didn't. He weaved from side to side separating the man smell from the horse smell until he had it all plotted in his mind just where those intruders were. He then dropped back down on to all fours and turned to

114

climb discreetly up and around through the northward forest. For a half hour Emmett could hear him whimpering and snarling and blundering through underbrush as he made his detour. When he was definitely gone on, the Texan raised his gun hand, rolled up his eyes, and said, "Lord'a'mercy; I thought he was goin' to rassle us f'sure. Doggoned mangy old critter anyway—with all the forest hereabouts why's he have to come traipsin' through here, anyway?"

"He's probably wondering the same thing about us," said Emmett, and whipped up off the ground as Matt came silently out of the westward trees. "You danged near got shot for a bear," he told his pardner.

Matt brushed the bear talk aside. "I saw the herd. I also saw Thompson and the others. They're down—"

"How many?" Demanded the Texan quickly.

"Thompson and four others. Five all told. They're down the hill where the trail goes right up through a regular glade without a tree on either side of it for at least a mile. They're pushin', but not hard, and one of the men was ridin' a lathered-up horse. I reckon that feller's been down their backtrail lookin' for pursuit. If he'd seen any they wouldn't be cruising along free an' easy like they are. They're about two miles from the pass, I'd judge."

"Well hell," growled the Texan. Where's Sheriff Miller and the other fellers? They're supposed to be closin' in from behind ain't they?"

Emmett nodded. "They're back down country somewhere, you can bet on that. Miller doesn't strike me as a feller who'd be seen if he didn't want to be seen. But that's not what's puzzling me right now."

Matt said: "Yeah. You and me both. If Miller is so far back Thompson's scout never even got wind of him,

115

and Mike's whole crew is up there with Thompson an' the herd—then who the hell are those four fellers up there in the pass?"

The Texan rolled his eyes. This evidently had not occurred to him until just now. Emmett also stood silent and thoughtful. Matt, who had obviously been worrying over this since seeing all the rustlers together down with the stolen herd, seemed to have an idea.

"Em; I couldn't get close enough to be sure, but I figure it just might be—"

"The Sioux!" Said Emmett quickly.

Now their companion's rolling eyes abruptly became very still. He stared hard at Matt and Emmett. "You mean," he softly drawled. "There's *Injuns* in these lousy mountains too?"

"That was an Indian boy your friend Thompson killed, Texas. There was a hunter camp of them down where you saw those stone rings." As he said this Matt looked from the Texan up where afternoon's reddening glow was softly mantling the twin sides of that upcountry pass through the mountains.

"Not my friend," stated the cowboy emphatically. "I took Mike's orders 'cause he was rangeboss, but he wasn't no friend of mine. In fact, outside of maybe Link, there wasn't a feller on the ranch who cared very much for Thompson, and that's a blessed fact." The Texan turned to also gaze upcountry. "The hell of that is, though—will those cussed redskins believe it; an' whether they do or not, just how are they goin' to feel towards whiteskins now?"

Matt grunted and dropped his gaze back to their immediate surroundings. "They'll feel about the same way you'd feel, Texas, if that had been your little boy Thompson shot. There's not that much difference between races."

"Well then, Mister Grady, I got a feelin' we ought to go back and join up with Sheriff Miller. How many o' them redskins did you say there was?"

"Twenty or thirty, countin' the woman too."

The Texan's jaw gradually closed hard. He stared straight at Matt, his expression turning both fearful and suspicious. But he didn't say a word, he simply turned to cross over where their horses were drowsing and lean upon his saddle seat gazing intently up towards the yonder pass.

"Scairt," muttered Matt.

Emmett nodded. "He's got reason to be. So have we. Maybe Blackie was melancholy the night his boy died, but that was twenty-four hours ago. A feller can build up to an awful hate in twenty-four hours, Matt."

"Under some circumstances twenty-four hours can be a whole lifetime, Em. When you've only got one son and you watch him die, it could be more than a lifetime because along with him goes all your hopes for the future. But we didn't shoot the boy, Em, and Blackie knows that."

"Sure; but if that's him waitin' up there in that pass there are three others with him. What do they know, Matt, except that whiteskins are comin' up towards them?"

Matt shrugged. He looked irritated. "There's no other way. We can't do like Texas says, go hunt up Miller. We're too near the pass to quit now."

"Who said anything about quitting?" Emmett muttered. "What we've got to do is get to those hunters before they lay their ambush for Mike and his pals. Get to them and keep them from doin' the one thing that'll set this whole blessed countryside aflame all over again like it used to be years back when redskins massacred whiteskins. And we've got to do it right now too, because within another couple hours it's goin' to be so dark in here a man can't see his hand in front of his face, which will be just right for pilgrims like us in strange country to blunder into that ambush an' get tipped over in Thompson's place."

Matt agreed. They went across and explained what they had in mind to the Texan. He glumly listened and afterwards, when they got astride, he glumly went along, but he neither approved nor disapproved their plan. All he said was that he never thought he'd get perforated doing the *right* thing; he'd always thought he might someday get picked off sticking up maybe a stage or some country store, if it ever came to where he had to do such a thing to keep eating.

"An' don't you two realize—we'll be right damned in between Thompson's gun crew and that redskin gun crew. Man; if a feller was to sit up all night figurin' a way to get someone into a pickle, couldn't no man in his right mind hope to ride away from, he couldn't do a danged bit better than we're doin' right now. Sometimes I wish I'd just stayed t'home down in Amarillo and worked for m'uncle in his blacksmith shop. I'd o' died barefooted in a bed with m'younguns all aroun' me, loaded down with m'years, 'stead o' get blowed to Kingdom Come up in these lousy mountains where a feller could lie till his clothes was out o' style before anyone ever come across his carcass. Well; lead on. Let's set out t'be big heroes an' get this over with."

They rode away from their rest camp bearing straight towards the yonder pass. Matt led because he knew the way.

15

THE ENTIRE WAY AS FAR AS ANY OF THEM COULD SEE was through trees which stood in staggered tiers, but Matt halted once to explain that shortly they would come to a place where the forest turned thinner, and after that they would be able to see the trail itself.

This proved true. The trail, when Emmett and the Texan finally saw it, appeared to be partially grown up in second-growth pine, but it definitely had at one time been a wide, broad clearing, obviously cleared by hand, which turned northward about where the three of them encountered it, and went off up through the forest towards that westerly notch they'd sighted earlier.

For the first time too, they could definitely hear lowing cattle. But the sound was distant and downhill. "Mile," muttered Emmett, listening intently. "Maybe a mile and a half." He looked around. It was turning shadowy where they sat back in the trees well away from the onward trail. "Matt; you better scout this place. Thompson might have a man out riding up in here."

But Matt shook his head. "Thompson's not worried about what lies ahead," he said. "What he's sweating over is just how far behind him the pursuit is. Come on."

They rode out upon the trail, looked fore and aft, turned upcountry and set their animals to the gradual, loamy climb. The sunlight was brighter out here. Also, as the land rose along towards its eventual top-out, the air got thinner and the skyline marched steadily down to meet them. When they were about a half mile southward Matt halted, turned his horse to halt Emmett and their companion the Texan, and to listen. It was now no

119

longer possible to hear cattle lowing.

"Where are those four riders from here?" Asked the Texan, looking carefully around.

Matt gestured carelessly on uphill, turned and went on another hundred yards, then he halted and dismounted, took out his Winchester and started to lead his mount on across off the trail into the deep forest. Emmett gestured for the Texan to do likewise. Later, when the three of them had their animals safely hidden, Matt poked a finger at the Texan's carbine saying, "Be sure it's loaded, Texas. We might have to fight off the whole Lakota nation up here."

The Texan watched Matt turn to go striding up through the trees. "Real joker," he mumbled to Emmett. "Got a real fine sense o' humor, your pardner. Be sure it's loaded . . . Me, knowin' what I know about redskins, and your pardner thinks he's kiddin' about empty carbines. Mister; if I had five sets o' hands right now I'd be prayin' for a loaded carbine in each set."

They followed Matt quietly. The way lay more steeply uphill now, until, coming abruptly out of the trees, they saw directly ahead of them, the high shoulders of wind swept and barren land. Here, the pass went straight between two slopes and on down the far side. Here too, the pass ran between those two opposing slopes for almost a hundred yards. The sun was shining out there, but not in the pass itself. It was very probable that the sun only struck directly down into that pass for only one hour each day, as it was passing from right to left across its zenith.

"Hey," breathed Emmett, laying a hand upon Matt's forearm. "Yonder's one of them." Both Matt and Texas turned in the direction Emmett indicated. There was a solitary lanky silhouette over behind some rocks up into the shadowy pass itself, perhaps four hundred feet distant. The man had a carbine tipped up against a stone wall at his back. He seemed to be drowsily keeping an indifferent vigil.

The Texan said: "Where are the other three?"

"If I knew that," growled Matt without taking his eyes off the sentinel up ahead, "I'd know what to do next."

"I can make a suggestion, Mister Grady—tuck tail an' get to hell out'n here."

Matt ignored the Texan. He kept studying that vague, shadowy silhouette up there, but because the sentry never moved nor fully exposed himself from behind the rock where he was loafing, Matt could make no positive identification.

"It's not Blackie," Emmett said. "It must be one of the others who run with Blackie though. He's dressed like a rangerider."

Distantly, borne upcountry no doubt by a rising breath of air, came the faint sound of tired cattle. At once the sentinel up in the pass became wide awake. He picked up his carbine, leaned forward looking down through the thin forest stand, and settled both elbows upon the rock in front of himself.

"We've got to make our move," stated Matt. "If we can hear the drive coming Thompson's crew can't be far behind. We've got to get this settled up here before any of them show up. Em; I'll leave my carbine here and walk up there. That one'll know where the others are. You and Texas stay here. I'll whistle you out if all goes well."

"An' pray for us if it don't," muttered the Texan.

Matt stepped out of the trees and halted. The sentry up ahead didn't look over towards him; he was

121

concentrating on the sounds of driven cattle, his head turned slightly away from the trail.

Matt strode across the cleared area with an easy stride. it was obvious from his bearing that Matt was reasonably confident. Suddenly the sentry catching movement from the edge of his eye, spun half around. Emmett saw Matt stop and raise his right hand, palm outward, in the age-old token of peace, of friendship. Emmett saw the sentinel lift his carbine and hold it two-handed as he stepped around his stone out into the pass. A vagrant sunbeam struck across the man's hatbrim-shaded features. Emmett heard the Texan gasp. He might have gasped himself, too, for that wasn't an Indian up there covering Matt with his cocked Winchester, *it was a white man!*

Matt evidently had made the same identification. He slowly dropped that upraised arm back to his side. The sentinel made a hard little gesture with his gun. "Walk on up here where I can get a good look at you," he said.

There wasn't any astonishment in the sentry's command. It was as though he'd been expecting someone about like Matt. Emmett, guessing what had happened, fought back a deep-down groan, turned and motioned for the Texan to come close.

"We out-foxed ourselves," he whispered. "That feller's no Sioux."

"Thank th' Lord," said the Texan fervently under his breath.

"There must be more to the gang of rustlers than just the men riding with Thompson. We should have guessed they'd have a watcher up here. Sheriff Miller said they would have, when we first met him about noon."

The Texan recovered, turned and craned out where

Matt was walking on up to the man with the gun. "Unless Matt can think real fast he's got his neck in a wringer."

Emmett stepped over, raised his carbine and dropped it into the crotch of a small tree. "Talkin' fast won't help," he muttered. "That feller'll know the men he's riding with. He'll know damned well Matt isn't one of them."

"What you calculatin' t'do?" Asked the Texan. "Man; you pull that trigger and these hills are goin' to sprout more gun barrels than you'n I can count."

Emmett said nothing. He had that armed man up there in the pass in his carbine sights. He didn't want to shoot because to do so now would stir up a tempest. On the other hand he had no intention of seeing that man gun down Matt or even march him off out of Emmett's sight. Perspiration ran down between his shoulder blades.

The Texan sighed, stepped across to another tree, knelt over there and also raised his Winchester. He wasn't the least bit in favor of fighting where they now were—between two factions of armed outlaws—but he'd at least hold up his end of things. Like Emmett, he kept his vigil and watched Matt walk right on up and stop a few feet from the stranger with the low-held, cocked gun. The air was thin, mirror-clear and acoustically perfect up there atop their rugged mountain. Without any effort they heard every word that passed between Matt and his captor.

"Who'n hell are you, anyway?" Demanded the gunman of Matt. "Where's your horse; how come you to be up in here?"

"One at a time," Matt answered. "I'm a friend of Mike Thompson's. You know Mike?"

Suspiciously and non-committally the gunman said, "Yeah I know him; what of it?"

"Well; he sent me on ahead to warn you—there's a big posse in these mountains."

Emmett and the Texan exchanged a look. Matt was thinking fast. If he'd taken a long chance it was also a fairly obvious one; since Matt's captor wasn't one of the Sioux hunters, then he probably was some ally of the rustlers.

The man said, "Big posse? Where? I been watchin' up here the last couple hours. I didn't see no dust. Didn't see no riders either, an' brother, I sure been watching."

"They're comin' in from the east, over where the mountains swing down this way. Comin' through the forest. Mike says for the other fellers up here to ride off eastward and keep close watch for 'em."

"*Mike* says," growled the outlaw, lowering his Winchester slightly. "Who the hell does Mike think he is—all of a sudden. He gets his pay for every lousy head he delivers to us an' that's where it ends. He don't boss no one an' he don't give no orders."

Matt shrugged, pushed back his hat and gazed southward where the sounds of lowing cattle coming upgrade were growing steadily stronger. "All Mike's tryin' to do is save things, that's all, feller. Anyway, since murderin' that Injun kid he's got a bigger stake than ever before." Matt swung to gaze off in the other direction. Emmett, watching closely, knew what Matt was looking for: Those other three horsemen. He was ready to jump his captor, turned careless now, but first he had to know there would be no interference from his captor's friends who had been in the pass but who were no longer there.

124

The outlaw settled his carbine butt into the dust at his side. He said, "That was a tomfool thing to do, shootin' that kid. Bruce told him to wait, that the danged redskins'd push on. Them Injun huntin' camps never stay in any one place long."

"Well hell," protested Matt indignantly, making it believable, "what was we supposed to do with the cattle—hang 'em on tree limbs until the Indians decided to move?"

The cowboy looked down country and frowned. "About this here posse; is Thompson plumb certain about that?"

"Why else would he send me dustin' it up here?"

The cowboy twisted to look northward beyond the crest of the pass and Matt swung. It was that same chopping little short jab he'd used to put Link down. It worked here even better; this man wasn't expecting anything like that. He went over sideways, struck the ground and rolled once. Emmett and the Texan sprang forth but as Matt scooped up the unconscious outlaw's guns he waved them back. Now the sounds of cattle were interspersed with cries of drovers and occasionally the sharp clatter of shod hooves striking over stone.

Matt dragged the unconscious man over behind the same big boulder he'd been leaning upon before he saw Matt. After that he remained in the deepening shadows a long time looking and listening. Finally, he ran northward to the break in the pass, stood there gazing down the pass's north slope for a spell, then whirled and hastened down where the Texan and Emmett were impatiently awaiting him.

"We're in worse shape than I thought," he barked at those two with the increasing sounds of driven cattle around the three of them. "Evidently Thompson cuts out the cattle to be rustled, drives 'em to some isolated part of old Farraday's range, meets one of these rustlers, tell him where the critters are, then the thieves take over. Yonder, down the other side of the top-out, is a campfire on a plateau part way down the slope. I counted three men sittin' around down there. My guess is that as soon as they hear the herd comin', they'll ride on up, pay Thompson off and take over."

"Only three," began the Texan, and got cut off before he could say any more.

"Only three *down at that camp*. There's at least another three with Thompson. And Mike—don't forget him. He's maybe got more reason to put up a fight than the rustlers. Folks hang fellers for murder, Texas. Even in Montana."

The Texan counted on both hands. "That's seven guns against our three guns," he pronounced. "Where the devil is Sheriff Miller?"

"The U.S. army'd be better," mumbled Emmett under his breath, then, louder, he said, "Matt; what've you got in mind?"

Matt retrieved his carbine, cocked his head in a listening posture, then shrugged. "We can't do much here, Em."

"How about makin' a stand in the pass?" Asked the Texan. "We could stop their drive cold."

Matt looked at the Texan. "You ever been caught between two fires?" He asked. "Well; I have, and I don't aim to be caught that way again. Once, a man can be lucky. Twice—no. The minute we try anythin' in the pass those fellers down the other side'll come boilin' up. Then from southward'll come Thompson and *his* men."

The Texan nodded and fell silent. Emmett also gauging the closeness of the oncoming noise as Matt had done,

126

said, "Scatter the cattle, Matt. We can do it on foot pretty easy. Range cattle run from a man on foot quicker'n they run from a pack of wolves. All we got to do is make blessed sure Thompson an' his friends don't spot us."

"Hey, boys, that's it," exclaimed the Texan exuberantly. "It'll keep the whole flock of 'em riding the slopes roundin' 'em up again until Miller gets up here."

"Or until night comes," agreed Matt. "Pick up your carbines. Let's go."

They paused only briefly while Emmett asked about that man Matt had knocked out. "No worry there," Matt answered dryly. "He'll be sleeping for another hour anyway. I hit him with everything I had."

They faded out in the shadowy forest on the west side of the trail, waiting for the point rider to heave into sight and behind him, the first shaggy backs and wicked horns.

Sunlight lay in red patches through the forest now. It was getting along towards evening. Dust roiled the uplands air. The herd was fast approaching.

16

EMMETT CAUGHT FIRST SIGHT OF MOVEMENT AND pointed it out to the others. A man on a laboring horse was passing in and out of the trees. He sat twisted in the saddle looking back.

"It ain't Mike," mumbled the Texan, and gripped his carbine. "Do we let him go past?"

Matt said, "Yeah; let him get up into the pass. And remember, don't yell or wave your arms. Just step in front of a critter and duck out of sight again. Let only the cattle see you, otherwise . . ." Matt raised a rigid forefinger and drew it from left to right across his throat.

That point rider emerged into the open, paused to squint up towards the pass, then knee his horse out again. Neither Matt nor Emmett knew this man, but he was young and rough looking and wore his handgun lashed to his right leg. He was obviously no ordinary cowboy.

They let the man slouch on past. Behind him a hundred feet came two big puffing steers, much too fat for this kind of work, their eyes red and inflamed from dust and arduous climbing, their wide horns faintly glistening in the murky red glow of the forest shade.

"Careful now," muttered Emmett, eyeing those horns, as Matt glided out to the very fringe of forest and braced to step out into the sight of those aggravated beasts.

Far back came the curses and the cries of other men. This near the top-out, after all the climbing they'd done, the cattle were logy and leg-weary. Matt was counting on this; except for the point rider leading the way, the other rustlers would all be far back urging straggling cattle ahead, no small feat when the cattle were as greasy fat and winded as this bunch was.

Matt moved around a tree, moved where both the steers couldn't help but see him, and stopped. The nearest critter spotted him at once and threw up its head to stare. The other critter didn't catch sight of Matt until he deliberately flapped his arms. This animal then quickly raised and lowered his horns and gave a startled snort. That was all it took for the first one to spook. He shied violently, struck his travelling companion, and Matt gave a short lunge at them both which completed the rout. Both big steers lifted their tails, turned off the trail and bolted eastward through the trees. Matt at once

128

stepped back out of sight again.

The next cattle were a hundred feet back. They came plodding along with uphill grunts of effort. They were traveling six or eight abreast, filling the trail, which was much better for Matt's purpose. But now Emmett and the Texan got in behind the last bank of trees lining the trail too.

They let the cattle get almost up to them. Emmett, in fact, was so close to a big old puffing heifer he could have poked his carbine out and tickled her ribs with it. He made a low whistle to catch this red-eyed beast's attention. When she threw up her head he ducked low and jumped out from behind his tree at her. The reaction here was swifter than it had been with the horned steers. The heifer gave a bawl of fright and hurled herself away from Emmett into the other animals pressing close around her. Matt and the Texan then sprang out also. The cattle saw them less than twenty feet away swinging their arms and rushing forward; they reacted as the startled big heifer had also reacted. They slammed down to a stiff-legged halt causing a pile-up behind them, then, as the men whipped in closer, the cattle plunged left and right in a wild and violent effort to get away.

Up to now these beasts, worn down and winded from their labors, had been hanging back. Now, in a twinkling, they panicked, breaking clear of the trail to the east and to the west, crashing into the forest, trampling one another, caroming off big trees and floundering over smaller trees in their blind terror. Fright among cattle being very contagious, the following animals also panicked although probably they didn't see the reason for their leaders' fear.

Emmett restrained the Texan, who would otherwise have rushed across the trail to complete this explosion of terrified animals, and dragged him back with Matt into the westward forest. The Texan was panting, his eyes were bright from excitement, from triumph, and only when a man bawled out a string of furious curses up where the point rider had gone, did he get cautious again and follow Matt and Emmett in a quick run back through the westward trees.

Cattle, no longer simply lowing in protest, now bawled in fear and panic as they blundered off through the eastward forest. As was the way with terrified critters, the more they ran, the more tree limbs slapped them, underbrush stung their tender noses and eyes, the greater became their stupid fright. They went off in little bunches, or separately charged almost blindly eastward.

The point rider appeared mercilessly rowelling his tired mount. He swung to the left of the trail in a wrathful attempt to get up and around the stampeding cattle and turn them. From farther back where a few remaining drag-end critters came up and halted in uneasy bewilderment, appeared more horsemen. Emmett, down on one knee between Matt and the Texan in the opposite direction those men were staring, pointed out one rider.

"Thompson," he said, over the tumultuous bedlam of cursing men and terrified, stampeding cattle. But they had only a very brief look, then Thompson, like the men around him, rushed pell-mell into the yonder trees. They left no one with the drag-end beasts back down the trail. Emmett tapped Matt's arm and jerked his head. The three of them arose, turned downhill and worked their way wraith-like through the gloomy trees until they were on the flank of those head-up, sniffing cattle down there, Clearly, tired as these beasts were, they were also skittishly on the brink of bolting. Emmett led out. Off through the eastward forest they could easily distinguish the yells and wild curses of the mounted men. Any danger of discovery down here was remote. Emmett ran out upon the trail directly in the face of the cattle. Matt and the Texan did the same. They were seen instantly. With a sudden sharp bawl, the startled cattle turned directly about and went bolting back down the trail in the direction they'd just come uphill to reach this spot.

Somewhere up near the pass a man's flat, booming call sounded. Emmett spun and raced for the trees. The Texan, broadly grinning, followed him. Matt, also following paused near the first tree he encountered to try and spy that man. He failed.

When the three of them were back together again Emmett smiled and Matt wagged his head. "It's not going to take 'em long to come together now; the ones from down the other side of the pass heard all the ruckus and came up. That's what the shout was about up in the pass."

"As long as they don't find their knocked out friend," speculated Emmett, "they'll likely figure it was a lion or a bear that caused the stampede."

Matt wasn't convinced. "I sure hope you're right, Em. Let's get back up to higher ground around the pass somewhere. If it takes 'em as long to round up their beef as I think it will, we're all right. If not . . ." Matt lifted his shoulders and dropped them, turned and went striding northward back through the trees towards the yonder clearing up where the slot through the hills lay.

Dust lay heavy in the pass, not so much from the stampede as from angry horsemen having just spurred up through there. No sign was visible where those riders had gone but Matt and Emmett were sure they'd rushed down into the eastward forest to join in trying to turn back the stampede.

Matt took them far back westward before he'd risk darting on across the clearing up into the boulders lining the rim. After that, though, it was relatively simple to make their way through the roiled atmosphere back down near the west side of the pass.

Sunlight lay darkly upon the forest downhill from where Matt halted finally, in a field of big boulders. From this high eminence they commanded a better view, actually, of the distant prairie than they commanded of their immediate surroundings. The forest hindered their view up close, but they could follow the progress of the rustlers easily enough by both dust rising above the trees, and also by the shouts and roared out curses.

"They won't get far now," Emmett stated. "Even if they get 'em rounded up an' back on the trail, they'll never be able to push 'em much farther than that plateau down the far side. They've got some tuckered horses on their hands and some cattle that'll be plumb run out."

The Texan eased down with his carbine across his knees and smiled. "Easy as fallin' off a log," he murmured. "Sure glad I thought o' that."

Matt grinned and also eased down. "Then think of something else to help us right now," he said, still grinning into the Texan's eyes.

"Oh; you mean Sheriff Miller an' the others," exclaimed the Texan casually, with a little careless flick of one hand. "Nothin' to sweat about on that score, Mister Grady. They'll probably hear all the commotion an' come hastenin' right along. Just relax."

"No," said Matt softly, still grinning. "I wasn't thinkin' of Dave Miller, Texas. I was wonderin' what Thompson's crew is going to think when it stumbles on to three saddled horses down there tied in the underbrush." Matt lifted an arm and followed out the southward and eastward noise of men and cattle down country. "Maybe you better figure something out for that mess, too, Texas." He stood up and turned towards Emmett. "We better get higher in these rocks. If those confounded critters had kept going due east we wouldn't be in too bad a position, but they didn't, they dropped southward. Are still droppin' southward. Those damned rustlers'll see our saddle stock sure, Em. And that'll sure take care of their thinking maybe a cougar or a bear spooked their herd."

The Texan jumped up. "Maybe if we hurried we could get down—"

"Forget it," Emmett said shortly, and turned on Matt. "All right; we couldn't win every point could we? So now we sit down up here and keep guard to make damned sure neither Thompson or his friends get through that pass."

Matt looked off in the direction of the continuing tumult and back again. "That's about the size of it, Em. Except that we had this figured wrong, though, I reckon we could have taken Mike Thompson easy enough. He's a bigger damfool than he is anythin' else."

Emmett looked doubtful about that. "How long you reckon Mike's been running his little rustling business on the side, Matt? If I was to make a long guess I'd say from the looks of this uphill trail he's sent a lot of animals over it to his buyers at the pass. If he's dumb, then I'd say he's dumb like a fox."

Matt wouldn't agree, but he didn't like arguing, so all he said in rebuttal was: "Yeah; so smart, Em, that today's probably his last outin' as a free man. Murderer, rustler—both hanging offenses, providing he lives to

133

hang. I don't call that bein' real smart."

The Texan, listening to this little exchange, screwed up his face and cogitated. He eventually arrived at his own decision, no doubt, concerning Mike Thompson, but he never got a chance to expound it. Down the hill a short distance a quiet man on a sweaty horse suddenly appeared right out of the forest. They all saw him. He sat with both hands upon the saddle horn quietly gazing around. First he made quite certain the southward trail was empty. Then he speared the westward area with his assessing stare, and finally he turned to gaze up through the pass. Until he did that, neither Matt nor Emmett remembered the knocked out man over in the yonder rocks. Now they remembered him, though, because that horseman down there abruptly turned, walked his horse into the slot, hauled up and swung down. From behind the boulder where Matt had dragged him, the wobbly, disarmed outlaw came unsteadily out, with one hand groping along in front and the other hand cupped around his swelling jaw where Matt had sledged him.

"What in the hell happened to you?" The mounted man demanded in a calm but very cold tone of voice. "That's why I came back—you were supposed to be watching up here."

"I was," mumbled the unarmed man. "Some lousy brush popper Thompson sent up here to warn me about a posse or somethin', caught me flush on the jaw."

The horseman stiffened. "Posse? What posse?" He sharply asked.

"I dunno; probably that feller was one of 'em. All I know is that he warned me—then slugged me." The injured man turned his head in bewilderment. "Where are the cattle; what'n hell's happened?" He asked.

"Stampede within a hundred yards of the pass,"

134

explained the horseman. "We figured it was some wild critter that spooked 'em. Now—I'm not so sure." The horseman turned completely around and back again. "This feller who hit you—what'd he look like?"

"I didn't pay much attention. Husky feller, dark, sort of Mex lookin' or maybe like a half-breed. What's the damned difference? Listen; if there really is a big posse in these hills we better abandon the cattle and ride for it."

The horseman though was not so easily upset. His cold gaze clung to the injured man. "Have you seen any dust?" He asked, and when his friend shook his head the horseman spat, looked southward, looked easterly where the stampede was losing its momentum, and said, "There's no big posse. If there was we'd have heard from it by now."

The other man, with reason to remember Matt, said, "Well; that feller who hit me wasn't no ghost, I can tell you that."

"One man with a hard punch is no big posse," retorted the horseman, and turned to mount up. "You better find your guns and do some scouting. The boys'll be herdin' the drive back up this way in a little while. I'd like to get them down on to the plateau before dusk. Make sure there's no one in the rocks around here." The horseman turned and quietly rode back down into the forest. Emmett and Matt, watching this man, could not restrain their grudging admiration. Whoever he was, that rustler was as cool and collected as though there had been no stampede.

"That one," stated Matt, "is more deadly than ten Mike Thompson's—whoever he is."

135

17

THEY KEPT THEIR VIGIL WHILE BELOW THEM IN THE slot where the pass ran its full distance between two upthrusts, that unarmed man went growlingly around searching for his weapons. For a while, because now the herd had been effectively halted and was being turned uphill again, they didn't heed that wobbly sentry down there except casually.

"What the devil's keeping Miller?" Asked the Texan, getting edgy as the rustlers began converging upon the pass with their subdued herd. "He must have quit comin'. "

Emmett wasn't too concerned about the sheriff or those other Farraday men. For one thing, he had faith in Sheriff Miller. For another thing, when that same icy-eyed, dead calm rider appeared upon the downhill pass again, in full view as before, he forgot all about the sheriff; that stranger affected him with the same chill of foreboding he affected Matt with.

Two more riders came forth from the trees. Both were riding head-hung, worn-out horses. One of them got down, gazed at his mount and sadly wagged his head. He said something to his pardner and the calm man, but only his pardner answered. The calm man was finished with his uphill study and was now gazing down the dusty but empty trail. He spoke. One of those men with him turned and started riding back downhill.

Matt eased in beside Emmett, got flat down and watched. It was shadowy down where that rider sat beside his dismounted companion. "I've got a bad feeling," Matt murmured. "I figure we ought to knock that man over right now. He's trouble for us ten ways from the middle." As he said this Matt pushed his carbine across the rocks making a little abrasive sound that brought the Texan's face around.

"You're a hell of a one to be accusin' Mike Thompson of murder, Grady. If you pick that feller off it'll be just as bad as Mike done."

Emmett frowned but withheld comment. He knew Matt Grady far better than the Texan did. Matt might believe killing that man down there was what he *ought* to do, but he'd never do it in cold blood, so at least for now, the horseman was safe.

Another rider came pushing on out of the forest. This one though only dropped a casual look upon the calm man, and swung to the right as though to push right on up into the pass.

"Hold it," said the calm man, when he and the rider were even. "I'll stay at the point this time. You go back and help the others get the critters back on the road."

The cowboy kept staring up where the sentry was. He seemed to want to dispute those orders. In the end, though, he hauled his horse around and went back into the trees.

Now the calm man turned and eased his horse out northward. Matt and Emmett watched him carefully from their hiding place in the rim rocks. When he got even with the unarmed sentry he halted, leaned forward and asked the man on foot if he'd found his guns yet. The sentry replied that he hadn't; he then said he couldn't understand what was happening. The mounted man sat his horse for a cold moment gazing downward. He made no offer to explain; he said nothing at all for a long while and Emmett, as far back as he was, could feel a sudden dread in his stomach.

Without a word the mounted man reached under his

coat, palmed a .45, flipped it to bring the hammer into full cock, then dropped it forward. The unarmed outlaw's head suddenly whipped around. He'd heard that sound through all the other increasing sounds where men were profanely working cattle through a forest. Emmett couldn't see the unarmed man's expression because the man's back was to him but he saw the quick lifting of his shoulders, saw the way his body sang up taut just one second ahead of the gunblast.

The unarmed man went over backwards with a scream choked off in his throat. Matt let off a ragged breath and reached convulsively for his holstered .45 The Texan, also stunned and jerking upright to see better, bumped Matt's arm. In that intervening fraction of a second Emmett recovered from his shock, reached forth and held Matt's gun hand in an iron grip.

"Don't," he growled. "It won't help the other one— he's dead. But it'll sure give us away."

Matt didn't cease trying to draw until that mounted man put up his weapon, turned his horse without another look at the man he'd just murdered, and booted the animal over into a choppy lope straight down the trail where other horsemen, and the first of the run out cattle, were beginning to appear.

"Cold blooded murder," gasped the Texan. "Never even give him a reason—just shot him down."

Matt finally relaxed. As Emmett removed his restraining hold Matt looked at him. "I told you, Em. I shouldn't have held off; I should've emptied his saddle the same way he just killed that other one. He's got ice water for blood, that one."

The rustlers came together down there with dying daylight staining them dark hues. The calm man was giving orders and gesturing. He acted no more like a man who had just committed murder than a block of ice might have. Downhill a cowboy appeared pushing a jaded horse. Matt and Emmett heard this new arrival call sharply to the calm man.

"Bruce! Hey Bruce! Forget the damned cattle there's a band of riders comin' up at us from southward!"

The outlaws, slouched and weary before, now whirled straight up in their saddles craning around where the newcomer was hastening forward. When he got in among them, still more men came out of the trees to converge. It was no longer possible to hear what was being said down there, but the actions of those men was plain enough. Most of them wanted to quit the country right now, but the one called Bruce, evidently the leader, prolonged this meeting by asking questions of the scout. This man turned and pointed back down the trail. This much Emmett and Matt and the Texan could easily understand: Sheriff Miller was coming up fast. What they strained hardest to hear, and failed to hear, was what Bruce had to say. Whatever it was, though, did not entirely alleviate the sudden concern of the other outlaws. There was a brief, violent argument. Bruce, outnumbered, gave in. He turned his horse and started up towards the slot again.

Matt lifted his carbine. "Now," he said to Emmett and the Texan. "Leave Bruce to me."

But the other renegades, more excitable, pushed on ahead. When they got up close enough to see that dead man sprawled out there in the dying day, Bruce was near the end of the column. The foremost rider cried out and pointed. Others crowded up, saw the dead man, and began to frantically duck away as though they thought someone in the pass or beyond it had shot their companion.

Matt raised his carbine, hunted for Bruce, didn't find him, and slashed a shot down towards another man; but this man was moving and the light was poor. Matt's bullet struck a distant slab of pure granite, bounced off skyward and made a chilling whistle as it sped away.

At once the outlaws wrenched around to race for cover. One of them quit his lagging horse in a wild leap and ran over into the nearest rocks across the pass. Emmett fired at this man driving him straight down. The Texan too got off a shot. Somewhere down in the forest a man cried out. Whatever it was he said was indistinguishable through the sudden apprehensive bawling of the cattle farther back. Matt looked hard, but the nearest he came to finding the outlaw leader was to locate his riderless horse standing next to a big fir tree looking thoroughly tired and bewildered.

"That'll hold 'em," said the Texan grimly, levering up another charge in his Winchester.

"It'll do more'n that," growled Matt. "It'll let Miller know we're still up here alive an' kickin'."

"All the same he'd better hurry," muttered Emmett apprehensively, taking a quick, long look out and around. "When they get over being surprised it's sure to occur to 'em they can get up into these rim rocks too, an' if they do that, this isn't goin' to be any one-sided fight."

"One-sided," croaked the Texan. "Man; they still got a lot of firepower opposed to us down in them lousy trees."

Matt abandoned the conversation, sank lower into the rocks and poked his carbine out. It was dusk now, shadows intervened to help his enemies down in the forest, silence settled and after a while even the dumb brute bawling dwindled as the cattle, no longer being pushed here and there, meandered off in search of a pine needle bed.

This was, in Emmett's view, the dangerous time. He inched farther down into the rocks to be closer to his companions. "We better get moving," he suggested, "and keep moving. Any time armed men on the peck get as quiet as those fellers are it means they're up to something."

"Like what?" the Texan inquired. "You mean skulkin' up on to us in these yere rocks?"

"Exactly like that," affirmed Emmett, and turned to Matt who was intently watching the down slope country. "What say, Matt; should we head east or west?"

Matt looked around. "Try goin' straight up," he growled. "Em; use your head. We can't leave this place. If we do, and if we don't shoot each other when it's dark later on, why then Miller'll shoot us. No; we stay right where we are."

"Matt, dammit," protested Emmett. "They're too blamed quiet. They're sneakin' up on to us for sure."

Matt didn't answer. He raised his carbine, took a long rest upon the side of a boulder and fired. Someone down in the forest gave a big bound and a startled squawk. Instantly two lances of muzzleblast lashed straight back towards Matt's. As Matt ducked back the Texan said: "What you aimin' at down there?"

"Nothing," answered Matt, glancing past at Emmett. "There's your answer, Em. They're not tryin' to get up into the rocks with us. Not yet anyway. Until it's so dark we can't see them run across the opening between the forest and the rim rocks, they won't try to get up here either."

Emmett subsided and so did the Texan, but Matt

crawled around until he could see the forest from around the base of another big boulder. There wasn't a sound down there. Even the loose horses had been coaxed out of the trail and the cattle, deciding something had distracted their herders, were going back down the trail again, in their dim minds following only two instincts, the urge of homing animals, and the motivation of hunger. In pine woods country turpentine sours the soil to where not even buffalo grass will grow.

"Hey up there in the rocks," a man cried out from back in the trees. "You fellers the law?"

Matt looked around at the other two and shook his head. None of them answered. Time passed. Evidently those trapped men down in the forest had appraised their situation and had found it far from enviable with gunmen in front and a posse moving up from the rear.

"Hey you boys in them damned rocks," boomed out a different, deeper and more resonant voice. "Listen yere—whether you're lawmen or not, how'd you like a thousand dollars apiece? All you got t'do is get on your horses and drop down the far side of the pass an' keep on ridin'. That's all. We'll send a man out right now with the money—all you got to do is say how many of you there are so's we'll know how much to send."

Matt called dourly back. "You ought to write a book, feller. You're sure windy. As for the money—you don't have enough. But if you really want out, why just send Bruce up here to us. If we get him we'll give you a five minute head start—on foot?"

Someone down there angrily fired towards Matt's voice. Matt didn't move but he fired off three rounds as fast as he could lever up and tug off. If there had ever been any doubt about the willingness of the men in the rim rocks to fight hard that grim resistance stilled it. But

142

it also decided the pinned-down men in the forest on their course of action. They began systematically firing, moving in and out and firing some more. Clearly, until the pass was open to them, they couldn't even think of escaping, and every minute was valuable too.

The sounds of gunfire grew and echoed. Matt fired occasionally but without tangible targets he was loath to waste bullets. Emmett and the Texan, behind their respective rocks, also entered the battle. It see-sawed back and forth without any visible advantage for nearly five minutes. Bruce's outlaws then began a slow advance right up to the final fringe of trees. They had obviously decided to rush the rim rocks as soon as it got dark enough for their chances of getting across the intervening cleared space to be increased from what they had been, as long as daylight lasted.

Matt crawled back where Emmett and the Texan were. "Watch close," he told them. "When the shadows settle down they're coming."

One man among the outlaws had evidently emptied his Winchester and had no more cartridges for it; he was using his .45 and the sound was entirely different.

Emmett spotted movement, trailed it, attempted to anticipate it, and missed by a yard when he eventually fired. But he did accomplish one thing; he drove his startled target belly-down behind a mighty old bull pine.

The Texan too had his brief moment of limelight. That booming voiced man among the outlaws down there, was obviously from his talk another Texan. Matt's and Emmett's Texan called to him saying he was a disgrace to Texas and that probably he wasn't a real Texan anyway because he didn't have the guts to step out and fight. The outlaw almost accepted this challenge, but not quite. Someone nearby spoke sharply to him so all Matt's and Emmett's Texan got back by way of reply was a reviling curse and two forty-five blasts. This at least identified for the pass's defenders who was down to using his gun belt now.

The Texan hooted at his counterpart among the rustlers and fired low in the direction of those two pistol shots. He got back another two, blazed away once more, and afterwards the private feud ended, probably because the outlaw Texan had to take time out to reload.

It bothered Matt that Miller hadn't come up yet. He'd originally made his play to hold the renegades on the strength of that report brought up to Bruce by one of the rustlers that there was a posse approaching. He had made a close calculation that if he and Emmett and the Texan could prevent the outlaws' escape just a little while, Miller would arrive to put Bruce's men between two fires. Now though, dusk was fast settling even in this uplands country, and soon the outlaws would make their charge. Unless Sheriff Miller arrived and took part in this battle within the next fifteen minutes, he might just as well never arrive at all.

Emmett seemed to be entertaining some similar ideas for he put his head down close and said, "Matt; without our horses we can't get away from them without one hell of a lot of luck. Miller better hurry up."

Matt said nothing.

The gunfire began to take on a dark glow each time someone fired. Shadows crept up like sooty silk and layered even the rim rocks. The forest turned more gloomy than ever. Even the cleared-off trail steadily darkened as sunlight gradually failed. Farther down, where no sunlight shone any more at all, night was thickening upon the land.

Suddenly all the gunfire from the forest stopped. The

silence became as loud now in its own way as the gun thunder had been. The Texan scooted down and methodically began to plug fresh loads into his guns. He lay the .45 upon a little rock close to hand. He looked at Matt and Emmett, making identical preparations, and said, "Sure been interestin' knowin' you fellers. If I get to hell first I'll stoke up the fires an' have a pot of java waitin'." He grinned.

Emmett raised up to risk a look around. It was safe; no one saw him, at least no one fired at him. He sucked down again, took up his Winchester and waited. Next to him Matt did the same.

18

UNEXPECTEDLY, A FIERCE AND SLASHING BURST OF gunfire erupted off in the eastward forest. Matt and Emmett, caught totally unprepared, stared at the blinding, swift-fading scarlet flashes. The Texan, never at a loss for words under any circumstance, said, "Hey; what the devil! Look yonder—whoever that is, they're firing westward into the trees where them cussed rustlers are!"

This was the truth. Matt relaxed and ran out a rough sigh. "About time," he said to Emmett, over the bristling renewal of battle. "Miller finally made it."

Miller may have made it as Matt surmised, but the outlaws, appraising this fresh attack, saw immediately that they were outnumbered by the advancing attackers, and that furthermore, these were no ordinary uplands fighters, for the moment they fired they faded from sight and left no targets for the attacked outlaws to fire back at. There was only one course left and Bruce's men took

145

it. Without any yelling they suddenly burst out of the forest running hard for the same rim rocks where Emmett and Matt and the Texan were holed up. Red flashes of flame sprang straight at the holed-up men holding the pass.

Matt yelled at his companions: "Let 'em have it! Turn 'em back!"

He braced one shoulder against unrelenting granite and fired, levered and fired again. Emmett and the Texan also joined in this murderous, point-blank fight. Down in the forest, off to the westward, other riflemen joined in. To the east also, those other attackers ran ahead to catch Bruce's men from the rear.

An outlaw, hit hard from behind, flung up both arms and screamed. Another outlaw, legging it in a high, crooked sprint, took a Winchester slug head-on; it was as though he'd struck an invisible stone wall. He was knocked back and held motionless for a fleeting moment, then he too went down.

Bullets from back in the forest began cutting into the rim rocks. The Texan, victim of a near miss, cried out indignantly and profanely, his ringing denunciation carrying above all the other wild violence. The men to the westward bawled across to their eastward companions and after another moment the firing back downhill slackened off.

Matt saw a running man in a coat break clear of the dusky night less than a hundred feet away. The man had no carbine but in his right hand there was the pale glow of blued steel. Matt jumped up, dropped his own carbine and called ahead.

"Hey Bruce—right here!"

The oncoming man saw Matt at once. He skidded down to a fast halt, swung and fired. The bullet struck stone with a shattering impact. Matt's right hand dipped and arose in a blur of smooth movement. His fingers seemed to blossom blood red. The report of that shot sounded unusually loud because of the surrounding rocks which hurled the blast back downhill. Bruce sagged, half twisted under impact, fought to straighten up again, and went down when Matt's second slug hit him in the middle of the chest.

A man rushing along behind Bruce hooked both toes under the falling man and went down in a sprawl. He struggled frantically and groped with both hands for his lost six-gun. Matt called out, diverted this man's attention, and ran straight at him, arriving within three feet before the fallen man could spring up again. Matt put his cocked six-gun into the fallen man's face. All movement ceased. Around those two the night suddenly became still except for someone groaning and calling for help mid-way between forest and rim rocks.

"Thompson," said Matt softly, "if you know any prayers now's the time to say 'em."

"I ain't armed," gasped Mike. "You dassn't—it'd be murder."

"You'd know about that," snarled Matt, entirely unmindful that men were stepping forth from the forest on both sides of the trail. Equally unaware that Emmett and the Texan were gingerly rising up behind him to survey the sprawled men between them and their advancing allies. He didn't even hear Emmett call softly, saying, "Hey Matt; look out down there. That's too many fellers comin' out of the trees to be Miller and the Farraday riders." All Matt saw was the gray-twisted, sweaty face of Mike Thompson, made ugly by the raw fact that Thompson was facing certain execution.

"You'd know about murder, Thompson. Get up on to

your feet."

"Don't shoot for gawd's sake, Grady. Listen; it was an accident. I swear to you I never meant to—"

When Thompson suddenly stopped talking Matt saw his eyes bulge and roll to the right. A strong hand came slowly forth and slowly forced Matt's gun away from Thompson's face. Matt swung his head and snarled, "Leave be, Em. He deserves—" It wasn't Emmett. It was the Sioux range rider Black Cloud, called Blackie.

"You'd tell me to act civilized," the big Indian said to Matt, looking coldly at Mike Thompson on the ground half lying across the dead outlaw leader's form. "Then you'd better act that way too."

Matt resisted. "I'd never tell you any such a damned thing," he said. "This one should die."

"Yes, he should die. But if you, a half-blood, and I, a full-blood, are going to walk the white man's road, then we can't slide back to the blanket whenever it suits our purpose. The law gets this one."

"That was your son, Blackie."

"All the more reason for you to listen to me, Matt. Put up the gun, it's over. I said put it up!"

Emmett came down to them. The Texan split off though, and went in search of his companions who had been on the westward side with Sheriff Miller in the fight. Emmett reached down, caught swarthy Mike Thompson ungently and yanked him upright. He frisked the ex-rangeboss for hideout guns, found none, and holstered his own weapon as he twisted to see who all the other armed were around them poking among the dead outlaws and roughly caring for the injured ones.

Braid was there. So were a number of stalwart Sioux range riders Matt couldn't recognize in the settling night. Dave Miller walked up poking his .45 into its hip

148

holster. Dave squinted at the dead man, raised his eyes and said to Thompson: "Is that man's name Bruce Evitt?"

Thompson nodded without speaking. He was still badly upset by his near brush with death. Sheriff Miller turned, gruffly, called to two men nearby and sent them back for horses. "He's worth four thousand dollars dead or alive, Emmett. You're a rich man."

Emmett shook his head. "Matt gunned him, not me."

"Well," stated Miller facing Matt. "Then you're a rich man."

Matt's recent cold fury was still smoldering. He said, "To hell with that. I wouldn't touch anything about that man with a forty-foot pole. The money goes to a little friend I never got to know very well. This man's son; the one Mike Thompson murdered. All right, Sheriff?"

"Well sure, Matt," assented the sheriff soothingly. "Only if the lad's dead I don't see—"

"His father and mother aren't dead, Sheriff. His people aren't dead. You understand?"

Miller looked at Blackie, at Emmett, then at Matt. "Sure I understand. Now let's get these whelps tied on horses and head t'hell down out of here. I'm tired and thirsty an' hungry."

"One question," put in Emmett. "What took you so long?"

Miller made a little gesture towards Blackie. "He an' his friends smelt dust and rode over to investigate. They were on their way up through this same pass out of the country, but in a different direction. They saw what was happening, came back down where they'd seen us comin' on upcountry, and we joined forces. I took the Farraday men over into the westward trees, Blackie an' his bunch went over to the east. That way we had

149

Thompson an' his friends bottled up. Then, when Blackie opened up, that was the signal for us to come in too. What took so long? Nothing; it just *seemed* long to you boys." Miller canted an eye skyward. "It's not even eight o'clock yet." He turned away to go supervise the loading of the prisoners and the victims. Over his shoulder he said. "We found your horses; I'll have one of the leads fetch them up to you." He stopped, turned and beckoned. "Mike; come with me. You stay with those three and your chances of havin' breakfast tomorrow mornin' get slimmer an' slimmer."

Thompson hastened over to join Sheriff Miller. Matt let his shoulders sag. He glanced down, found his holster and carelessly dropped his six-gun into it. *"Dina sica,"* he said in Dahkota to the quiet Sioux standing between him and Emmett. "No good, Blackie."

"Plenty good," contradicted the Indian range rider. "He'll die. He'll pay, but like I said—there can't be two codes. Not any more."

Matt flared up. "How can you say things like that; he was your son."

"That's *why* I can say them, Matt," responded the Indian. "Because someday you'll have sons too. They can't grow up in a divided world. If you an' I don't back one law for all men, how can we expect our sons to? But they must, because their world is going to be even harder on them than our world was on us. Come on; the horses are here. You go back to Lodgepole."

"Where are you going to, Blackie?"

The Indian pointed northward across the high pass. "Other hunting lands maybe. I don't think it's time for the ranches to start hiring yet. Do some fishing, some hunting." He dropped his hand and softly smiled. "We'll meet again, Matt." He turned and walked off where his

150

friends were waiting.

Emmett went and got their horses. By the time he came back Matt was ready to ride. Sheriff Miller was already leading out down the back trail. Overhead, the moon was softly rising from behind an ancient saw-toothed ridge. The night was old and yellow and warmly promising like most late springtime nights are in the high country of Montana. The smell of burnt powder hung in the air but this too would pass, for all the violent things which occur upon the land diminish and die and the land goes on serenely everlasting, blind backdrop for the intrigues, the sufferings, the tragedies and the triumphs of men.

Matt and Emmett had little to say on the ride back. Sheriff Miller came back to ride with them once, just before they hit Farraday's range, but there wasn't a whole lot to exchange; Matt and Emmett already knew how Miller had gotten his unexpected but very welcome Indian allies. They knew, or had figgered out, some of the lesser details. So Miller went up to the head of his column and remained there all the rest of the way back into Lodgepole.

Where the Sioux split off Matt and Emmett paused to acknowledge their departure with a high-held pair of hands. Afterwards, they slouched along like Farraday's cowboys also did, and when they finally got back to town, put up their horses and got away from the others, they went up to the *Kalispell House* for a needed bracer or two. They were still there an hour later, nursing their thoughts and their quart of Old Overholt, at a gloomy corner table well away from the nighttime crowd, when Doc Farraday himself shouldered his way through to them, halted and reached for a chair.

"Mind if I sit down?" He asked.

Matt looked up. "Yeah I mind," he said, and sat there waiting.

Farraday let his fingers lie lightly across the chair's back without making any attempt to draw it out. "Dave Miller told me you'd likely be here."

"All right," stated Matt, still looking balefully from beneath his hatbrim. "You found us."

"I owe you boys an apology. I didn't believe all that talk; figured you wanted to get back at me."

"Get back at you?" Said Matt, easing back in his chair. "Mister Farraday I wouldn't spit in your middle if your guts were on fire. You want to know what I think of your kind?"

Emmett said softly, "Ease off, Matt. You've made bad mistakes too."

"Yeah. But never that got a kid killed."

Farraday now yanked out the chair and sank down down upon it uninvited. "Grady," he said, "I'm askin' help. I need two good men to replace Thompson an' Link. I need help rebuildin' a lot of goodwill I've let slide. Dave Miller says you two can give me that help."

Matt's eyes widened slightly. Even Emmett was surprised; this wasn't the same arrogant hard-eyed man they'd originally met at all. The cowman spread his hands atop the table and leaned forward. "Grady—rangeboss at top money. Ray—ranch foreman—name your wages."

Emmett looked at Matt then on across the table again. "Mister Farraday," he said conversationally. "Have you any objection to Indians hunting your uplands country?"

"No objection at all, Mister Ray."

"How about riders passin' through?" Matt asked, reaching for the bottle and the little glasses.

"I told you, Grady; I've been bad wrong. That'll be changed too. All I need is good men to lend me a hand."

Matt slowly poured, pushed a glass towards Farraday and pushed another glass towards Emmett. As he lifted the third glass himself, Matt said, "You just hired two men, Mister Farraday. Here's hoping it works out."

They all three drank.

We hope that you enjoyed reading this
Sagebrush Large Print Western.
If you would like to read more Sagebrush titles,
ask your librarian or contact the Publishers:

United States and Canada

Thomas T. Beeler, *Publisher*
Post Office Box 659
Hampton Falls, New Hampshire 03844-0659
(800) 818-7574

United Kingdom, Eire, and
the Republic of South Africa

Isis Publishing Ltd
7 Centremead
Osney Mead
Oxford OX2 0ES England
(01865) 250333

Australia and New Zealand

Bolinda Publishing Pty. Ltd.
17 Mohr Street
Tullamarine, 3043, Victoria, Australia
(016103) 9338 0666